BLOOD ON THE LAND

1844. British Army Officer Thomas Collins is sent to the fledgling Republic of Texas to meet the legendary President Sam Houston and negotiate terms for the British Empire's involvement in his country. What Thomas finds is a world of subterfuge and danger, and a republic scourged by an implacable and deadly enemy, the Comanche Nation. Collins' desperate fight for survival brings him into contact with Captain Jack Coffee Hays and his Texas Rangers, and ends in a lethal climax . . .

PAUL BEDFORD

◆

BLOOD ON THE LAND

Complete and Unabridged

LINFORD
Leicester

First published in Great Britain in 2012 by
Robert Hale Limited
London

First Linford Edition
published 2014
by arrangement with
Robert Hale Limited
London

A catalogue record for this book is available
from the British Library.

ISBN 978–1–4448–1884–0

Published by
F. A. Thorpe (Publishing)
Anstey, Leicestershire

Set by Words & Graphics Ltd.
Anstey, Leicestershire
Printed and bound in Great Britain by
T. J. International Ltd., Padstow, Cornwall

This book is printed on acid-free paper

1

For as long as God grants me time on this earth, I will never erase the memory of that first hellish scream. It was not until much later that I recognized it for what it was. A display of triumph at *my* discovery!

A dozen or so seemingly naked savages had appeared over the brow of the hill, and now tore towards us, levelling their bows. My horse reared in the face of such apparitions. Frantically trying to control him I turned to Buford and cried out,

'Do we fight or run?'

Regarding me intently through glassy eyes, he slid sideways out of the saddle: a metal tipped arrow was protruding from his throat, blood foaming from his mouth. Sheer terror gnawed at me, followed swiftly by the grim realization that I had no choice but to stand my ground. I flung myself out of the saddle, took the reins in my left hand and drew my Paterson Colt.

Aim for the horses, I told myself. *The horses!*

I pulled back the hammer, sighted rapidly down the nine-inch barrel on to the lead animal, and squeezed the trigger. The revolver bucked in my hand. Black powder smoke wreathed about me as the report rang in my ears. The .36 calibre ball poleaxed the horse, its front legs buckled, pitching its rider forward. The onset of action brought with it a measure of calm, as I told myself, 'That's one down, now . . . *Christ!*'

In one fluid motion the savage was on his feet. Desperately I cocked my weapon again. He was coming straight for me at a flat run, sunlight glinting off the knife in his hand. Resisting the onset of panic I stood fast, aimed and fired. The ball caught him square in the chest, the force of it stopping him in mid-stride. He crashed into the dirt again, and this time stayed down.

Then on to the next one. I had to keep firing! Again cock, aim, and squeeze. Another horse went down, stumbling and falling forward on to its now prone rider, blood pumping from a punctured artery.

Two chambers left, and they were still coming on.

So close now, that I was aiming for the riders. Swinging to the right, I fired up into a bronzed torso just as the warrior released a wickedly barbed lance. Triumph turned to horror, as the ball tore into his left breast, throwing him backward off his mount.

One chamber left!

Abruptly my left arm was almost wrenched out of its socket. I staggered and released the reins, dimly aware amongst the powder smoke and dust that my horse was no longer beside me. With no time even to look round, I squinted into the harsh glare of the sun, and found another target. Instinctively I fired up into the painted, hellish face looming over me. Blood and teeth sprayed out of his shattered jaw. Red flecks spattered over me.

Empty!

What now? The question screamed at me. All I could do was bluff. Searching for a fresh target, I cocked the revolver. It was hopeless!

But no, they were turning. The survivors were galloping off low and fast. They had had enough.

By god, I thought, *I'm still alive!*

* * *

The whole encounter had lasted less than two minutes. I was left stunned and swaying on my feet. Nothing in my time with the British Army had prepared me for anything like this. The area to my front resembled a slaughter-house. Two mortally wounded horses, their blood soaking into the earth, and four apparently dead savages. Were they, though? I needed to be sure. I had seen three take mortal wounds, and they were obviously no longer a threat to me. But the one lying prone, partly concealed by his mount, could have been biding his time. He was not to know that my revolver was empty, any more than his surviving comrades had. Glancing to my left I saw my horse threshing madly on the ground, the barbed lance that had brought it down still protruding from its belly.

Some yards beyond it my ill-fated guide, Buford LeMay, was lying sprawled in death, a look of stunned surprise etched on his face. Steeling myself, I moved over to the horribly suffering animal, grasped the lance shaft and yanked it from the gaping wound. Eyes bulging, the horse screamed with shock, and I realized that my body was quite literally trembling from the horror of what I had just done. But it was not over yet!

Gripping the primitive weapon tightly, I positioned myself over the prone body of the native, and stabbed downward with all my strength. A tremendous shudder shook his whole body as the blade penetrated his neck. He squirmed briefly like a trapped snake, then lay still again. Now I knew he was no longer a danger to me!

Without warning my legs buckled beneath me, and the ground came up to meet me with surprising force. I found myself slumped in the dust, profoundly shocked by my involuntary reaction. Of course I had experienced action before, but not of such immediate intensity as this. Gazing around at the carnage before me I felt the bile rise in my throat, and then the vomit spewed out with unstoppable force. I wanted to weep, but couldn't allow myself the luxury. I had no idea how much time remained before those strange and terrifying creatures returned. For some reason I was certain that they would.

★   ★   ★

My mind was struggling to cope, but I had to recover some measure of calm if I was to survive. The overwhelming priority was to reload my gun. I remained alive only because of that. The revolutionary weapon, a Holster Model percussion revolver, product of the Patent Arms Manufacturing Company, had only been offered for sale eight years earlier in 1836, and we were a long way from New Jersey. Not 'we' any more! Buford was dead, and I suddenly felt far too vulnerable sitting out in the open. Looking hurriedly around for any kind of cover I spotted a dry gully several yards off to my right.

I struggled to my feet, grabbed my saddle-bags and ran over to it. Chest heaving, I crouched down in my meagre refuge and began to reload. My hands were still trembling as a result of the assault, but I forced myself to concentrate. Even though I was well practiced, I faced a laborious, time-consuming task. Each of the five chambers had to be reloaded separately, firstly with black powder from a recharging flask, and then with a slightly oversized lead ball to ensure a tight fit. This charge was then compressed from the front of the piece, using a separate rammer.

'Damn it,' I snarled. Why was it taking so long? Suddenly, from some little distance away, I heard the sound of guttural voices.

'Oh my Christ, they're coming back,' I moaned. I wasn't *ready*! The percussion caps. I had to get the percussion caps on. Fumbling in my bag, I retrieved five of the red copper caps containing fulminate of mercury, and replaced the spent one on the bronze nipple at the rear of each cylinder. These too were a relatively recent invention, far more resistant to bad weather and a vast improvement over the flintlock mechanism. At last, with my hands black from powder residue and looking like part of a music hall act, I was ready to fight on.

* * *

The metal-tipped arrow slammed into rock, inches from my face, tiny slivers of stone searching out my eyes. Cursing, I turned, instinctively cocking and firing. The ball whined off mockingly into the distance, the owner of the shaft having disappeared from sight. This was a new development, in its own way more deadly than any frontal assault. The savages were obviously on foot and scattered around me. The land, now that I was away from the coast, consisted of endless rolling prairie. It was relatively featureless, but there were enough rocks and undulations for the surviving heathens to stay hidden. With time on their side they could keep on loosing their missiles at me with little risk to themselves.

It was time to take stock of my situation. I had food, ammunition, a Bowie knife purchased in Galveston and a small draw-tube spyglass in my saddle-bags. The proven short-range killing power of my revolver would prevent the savages rushing my position. On the negative side, the gully was too shallow to protect my upper body from arrows, and sooner or later someone would manage a lucky shot. Water! The water canteens were hanging from my saddle. *Bugger*, I thought angrily. *How could I forget that?*

The notion of liquid made me realize just how thirsty I was. A combination of fear and humid heat was causing me to sweat profusely. There were canteens on Buford's horse, but that was nowhere to be seen and so presumably now belonged to my attackers.

Having reloaded the empty chamber, I set to work deepening the gully, using the broad blade of the Bowie knife. If I was able to go down another foot or so I would almost be hidden from view. But that was easier said than done, for the ground was hard and, as an officer, I was unused to such toil. The knife did not make a good entrenching tool but fear provided the motivation. The sun burned down on my unprotected head.

Sweat poured from me. I wondered how long I had to wait before sundown.

Despite the heat I felt a sudden chill spread over me. For darkness would surely mean the end of my hitherto robust defence. The savages would be able to move in closer unseen, and then rush me from all directions at once. I would be lucky to stop one of them! The thought of my likely fate set me to jerking from side to side, frantically searching for any sign of my attackers. The shimmering heat haze seemed only to mock my efforts. It was not just the very real possibility of my dying in this god-forsaken wilderness; it was also the realization that all my efforts would come to nothing. Highly placed men at the heart of government had put their trust in me, and for what? For it all to end in some stinking hell hole miles from anywhere.

A thought occurred to me. My horse was dead, as was Buford, and they had presumably seized his mount. So why were they expending so much effort on me? Were they desperate to obtain my revolver? Possibly. I supposed that it could bring much prestige to its new owner. But a nagging doubt remained. Could all this have something to do with my mission to meet with the president?

★ ★ ★

Crouched in my earthy refuge, I eyed the rapidly disappearing pool of urine with distaste. It had not been easy having a piss without showing myself, especially as I also had a pressing urge to defecate. This I resisted strongly. To share this cramped accommodation with a fresh pile of faeces would have been intolerable.

Resuming my lonely vigil, I knew that my earlier supposition had been correct. Unless I became exceptionally careless, my adversaries would not make any further move against me before dark. I was alone, on foot and trapped. Dangerous yes, but only when

I could see my opponents. Until the light went they would leave the sun to do its work. June in Texas was apparently hot and very humid. My felt, wide-brimmed hat was lost, so I had pulled my cord jacket over my head and shoulders as protection against the burning orb.

Yet there was no escape from the relentless damp heat. My expensive shirt and breeches were soaked with sweat.

How do those devils out there stand this?

The sun had passed its zenith, but I still had many hours to wait before darkness fell. Part of me cried out for that relief, but I knew that its coming would only bring great peril.

If there was to be no choice I resolved to sell my life dearly, but who wanted to die aged thirty-one? With nothing to do but maintain my lonely vigil my mind began to wander. I knew it was happening, but somehow couldn't prevent it. I was drifting back to the origins of my current predicament. My instructions suddenly loomed so very large in my mind. I was to find Texas President Sam Houston and ascertain whether he would entertain Great Britain's economic and military involvement in his precariously weak and vulnerable republic. How I was supposed to achieve that in a land without roads or any discernible lines of communication was anybody's guess. At stake was a vast amount of cotton, needed to feed industrial England's insatiable demand. The parlous state of the country meant that I, a military man rather than a politician, had been entrusted with the thankless task.

2

My head lolled forward and that action woke me with a start. Had I really slept? If so, my behaviour was inexcusable, and would have brought serious repercussions down on any man guilty of it under my command. My reaction to that carnage must have been stronger than I had realized.

As I came to my senses I appraised my surroundings. I was glad that my assailants had been unaware of the lapse in concentration on my part. There was no visible activity, and so presumably they were biding their time. The sun was going down anyway, and darkness would soon cloak the land. Then I must surely meet my end. For how could I fight off the rest of those devils when I could not even see them?

As my eyes swept the landscape I tried to imagine which direction they would strike from. If they knew their business, as surely they must, they would mount a coordinated assault from all sides. They were definitely still out there somewhere. Of that I was sure!

As the sun slipped below my line of sight I shrugged into my jacket, careful to keep below the rim of the trench. I checked the load in each of the five chambers of my Colt, and jabbed the knife into the ground within easy reach.

I may very well die tonight, I thought grimly, *but I will take some of the swine with me*.

With a jolt I realized that darkness was closing fast. The total silence was eerie and disconcerting. It suggested that I was all alone, but of course I knew better. Was that a shadow or a man? The failing light was playing tricks on me. I could feel the tension building in my body. Although the sun was gone, I began sweating again. Muffling the Colt inside my jacket, I cocked the hammer slowly, but to my straining ears the noise sounded like an anvil strike. Anxiety coursed through me as I wondered, *How could they not hear that?*

It mattered not. They already knew exactly where I was. A noise from behind had me twisting anxiously around. As my heart leapt, my fevered mind responded with, *What in hell is that?* My arm swept forward in an arc, my revolver searching for a target. A bead of sweat trickled into my right eye, to be wiped impatiently away.

That sounded like a struggle: scuffling and grunting noises, but too far away for me to work out the source. Which meant it could be a feint to confuse me, and they were not coming from that direction at all. I swivelled back, just as a shape rose up from the ground in front of me like a wraith, a war lance stabbing forward. Instinctively I aimed for the torso and fired. The weapon roared in my hand. There was a powder flash, a scream, and the figure disappeared from sight. His lance clattered on to a rock in front of me. With my night vision gone, I was only dimly aware of another figure approaching on my right. With a blood-curdling howl the savage leapt at me, but I was ready. Hammer back, revolver levelled, I howled out, 'Come on you bastard,' and pulled the trigger. There was a dull thud. *Misfire!*

Frantically I fell back, desperately trying to cock the revolver, but I was out of time. The savage was so close that I could see his eyes flash in the blackness as he brought his axe down on my head. From the void behind him came an explosion of sound, and he was flung towards me like a child's doll. His momentum forced me to the ground.

As the man's dead weight collapsed on top of me the axe slammed into the earth inches from my skull. I could smell his breath; feel his body jerking on mine in an almost sexual passion. Grabbing his shoulders I heaved him off me, and staggered to my feet. Where in God's name was my revolver? Three more screaming apparitions appeared in front of me. Two to my left, one to my right, *but* there was something different about that one. I grabbed the Bowie from the ground at my feet, and felt the blast of pressure as a pistol ball flew past my right shoulder, embedding itself in soft flesh behind me.

'Don't just stand there, gut them,' bawled the figure in front of me. So saying he threw himself at one of the remaining natives. Pumping the long blade into soft flesh, he pulled upwards in one smooth, strong heave. His victim gave out an inhuman wail, his entrails flopping out on to the ground. Defensively I swept my own knife around in a wide arc, my wrist jarring painfully as it intercepted another weapon. Straining to hold it off, I was forced to give ground. The creature behind it had the strength of a berserker. I kicked out with my left boot, but missed and then his shoulder slammed into my chest, causing me once again to tumble back and down.

Lying stunned and helpless, I gazed up at my assailant, vaguely wondering why he did not strike. But he just stood there and coughed. Warm, sticky liquid cascaded on to my face, and I could hear screaming. Rolling on to my side, I retched and tried to wipe my eyes. I just wanted this to end.

'Lordy, lordy you scream like a woman. It's his blood, not yours, feller.'

I rolled on to all fours, sucked the cool night air into my lungs and looked around sheepishly like a dog awaiting another kick. The source of those words was standing a few feet away, using a powder horn to reload his recently discharged pistol.

'Reckon I just saved your hide, mister,' he observed, indicating the prone figure lying near me. A knife hilt protruded from the back of his neck. This was all just too much to take in. I pulled myself upright, and stood swaying slightly, all the time pawing at the sticky mess on my face. A sense of relief began to flood over me. I was alive! I had survived again, and I was alive. In large part because of the man before me. My mind was still reeling from the abrupt change in circumstances. All I could think of to say was a rather feeble, 'My name is Thomas Collins. Who are you?'

'Name's Bannock,' came the reply.

I waited, but nothing else was forthcoming. Slipping the pistol into his belt he moved slowly over to retrieve his knife. I peered at him through the gloom, trying to make out his features and feeling slightly unsettled. This man's arrival had undoubtedly saved my life, but I had a head full of unanswered questions and he seemed unnervingly calm. I tried again.

'You must forgive me. I am so very grateful to you. I was convinced those savages would finish me.'

'Comanches.'

'I beg your pardon?'

'They're Comanche warriors. The

21

most evil, dangerous sons of bitches in all of God's creation.' So saying, he wrenched his knife free of the warrior's neck. It came clear with a stomach-churning sucking noise that almost had me retching again. I expected him to wipe and sheath it, but instead he moved swiftly over to the Comanche whom he had shot behind me. Bending rapidly over the body he drew the blade across the man's throat. Blood oozed, but the body lay still.

'Just making sure. You'd best get your possibles together. We're moving out a ways.'

Still struggling to come to terms with the situation I asked somewhat lamely, 'Where to?'

'Over yonder,' he answered with a vague gesture. 'Away from all these cadavers.'

I could not argue with that. For some minutes I searched for my revolver, eventually locating it at the bottom of my trench. Even in the gloom I could feel Bannock's eyes upon me.

'You'd better reload that thing: it's the only reason you're alive.'

Anxiety coursed through me. 'Surely they won't return? Not after this.'

'Not normally, no, but there's nothing normal about this war party.'

'What do you mean?'

'Enough talk. Load it and let's go.'

That procedure took some time, but he waited patiently until I was ready. We did not have far to go. Bannock's mount was ground-tethered some fifty yards away. I imagined that we would then continue onwards, but that was not his intention.

'We'll cold camp here 'til sun up, and then head back to your battleground.'

Did I detect a hint of mockery in his tone? Possibly, but as he had just saved my life I did not bridle. Besides, I had too many questions to which I needed answers. 'How did you come by me? Did the gunfire alert you?'

My saviour had placed his saddle on the ground prior to rubbing down his horse. At my question he turned, his eyes flashing in the dark.

'I've been sat out here watching the elephant since I heard the first shots. Considering that you're not even from these parts you didn't do half bad.'

I was stunned and puzzled in equal measure. '*Elephant?* What elephant, and why didn't you *do* something?'

'I just did,' he replied laconically.

This was too much. To have endured that torment supposedly alone, and yet all the time under his scrutiny was beyond contemplation. He obviously sensed my disquiet because he took a step towards me.

'Before you get all riled up just listen, and listen good. I was one man; they were many, spread out around you. There was not enough cover to move in on them one on one. The only chance was to sit tight, and let them make their play. Once they closed on you I had them in one place, with the advantage of surprise.'

I made to speak but he carried on. 'Believe me when I say that they wanted you dead mighty badly. Comanches won't take casualties, and won't fight on foot. Their first charge cost them four dead, with one horse to show for it. Normally they'd have reckoned their magic was bad and hightailed it. But what did they do? They dismounted, and laid siege to you. So when it's light you and I are going to take a look-see.' He stopped and drew a deep breath. 'I ain't talked so much since my pa was laid to rest. I sound like an Austin politician.' He threw a coarsely woven blanket at me. 'No more talk, now we sleep.'

His assumption of command annoyed me. I threw the blanket to one side.

'Not likely!' Drawing my revolver again I said, 'This weapon is powder-fouled from firing. If the residue is not cleaned off it won't matter whether it's loaded or not.'

He shrugged and said nothing, but nevertheless watched attentively in the gloom as I performed my task. Only when it was completed to my satisfaction, did I lie down on the blanket and drift off to sleep.

★   ★   ★

Seemingly seconds later I came out of a deep dreamless slumber, only now it was light. The man I knew only as Bannock was none too gently booting my right leg.

'We're burning daylight, mister. Oh, and watching the elephant means seeing a battle, just so as you know.'

Groaning, I rolled over on to all fours, and then got groggily to my feet. I could do without explanations of colloquial slang so early in the day. Rubbing my eyes I focused, and took my first proper look at the man before me. He was tall, just under six feet, very lean and sinewy. He had unkempt sandy hair, fine stubble and reminded me of a pirate from the previous century. There was a powder burn on his right cheek, and an upper front

26

tooth was missing, presumably the result of some earlier conflict. All he lacked was a checked bandanna tied around his head. His expression in repose was hard, but not unkind. What held my attention were his eyes. As they held my own their intensity was disconcerting.

'Seen enough?'

'Forgive me,' I stammered. 'You saved my life, but this is the first that I have seen of you in daylight. After all, I wasn't lying in the grass watching you all of yesterday.'

A wry smile played on his lips. 'Fair enough,' he said, handing me what resembled a piece of leather. 'You'd better take a chew on this, it'll keep you going.'

Eyeing it dubiously I enquired, 'What is *this*?'

'Beef jerky,' came the reply. 'And without a fire that's the best vittles you're going to get for a while.'

'Surely a small fire won't be spotted in daylight?'

'I thought you were a brass hat? A little smoke might not be seen, but cooking smells travel for miles. Those bastards suffered grievous bad yesterday, and could have reported us dead just to save face. Let's not spoil things, huh?'

He was right of course. So I took a drink of water and tentatively bit off a small piece of jerky. Strongly smoked, it was actually quite pleasant. I turned and walked over to my saddlebags. Then I froze. Despite the warmth of the new day goose bumps formed on my flesh.

Spinning round to face him, I dragged the Colt from my belt, pulled back the hammer, and aimed it directly at his torso. Taking all this in, Bannock's eyes locked on mine, a calculating look playing on his face.

'Is this how you repay me for saving your hide?'

My aim did not waver as I snapped out, 'How do you know that I'm a soldier? I did not tell you, and nothing that I'm wearing is military issue.'

To my surprise he laughed loudly. 'You're a sharp one, ain't you?'

My finger tightened on the trigger, a fact not missed by his piercing gaze. He slowly raised his hands out in front in a placating gesture.

'All right, all right. Just ease off and I'll tell you. Christ, you British sure are touchy. General Sam ... sorry, *President* Sam Houston told me to keep an eye out for you. He knew that you would arrive in Galveston, but not when. I didn't make it in time, and it was just luck that I came upon your little shindig yesterday.'

Slightly chastened I eased the hammer down, but held my stance. 'But how could he know who and what I was? News could not have got to him quicker than I myself have.' I was confused and couldn't hide the fact.

Bannock shrugged. 'You'd best ask Sam about that. But think on this. Someone else knew about you as well.'

Waving back to the scene of my

ambush he continued, 'That was a murder raid with just one aim. To kill you at any cost.' Seeing me about to protest he gestured impatiently. 'Put that damn cannon away and follow me. I'll prove it to you.'

So saying he led his horse past me, blatantly ignoring my drawn weapon, and headed back to the scene of the previous day's ordeal. Standing there, feeling foolish and ungrateful, I was left with little choice but to follow. Carrion birds were already feasting on the bloated corpses, and were reluctant to move off. Gunshots were out of the question, so we shouted and threw a few stones until they flew off, protesting loudly. I had seen many dead bodies before, but the bile rose up in my throat yet again as I looked around the site of my last stand. Bannock moved carefully from body to body, quite obviously looking for something. Then, with a triumphant yell, he pointed to one of the savages sprawled near the trench.

'Now, look and listen. A Comanche

warrior is bred to a life of huntin' and warfare. He loathes Texicans, Mexicans and Apaches, in fact pretty much the whole human race. He will only make war in company with his own kind or, in the face of a large threat, with other tribal allies. His preferred time for raiding is during the Comanche moon, when the moon is full and the nights are lighter. It has always been so. Only last night was dark as a grain of gunpowder. Now, take a look at him.'

Looking down at the puffy face, I realized immediately that he was of mixed race with a smattering of European blood. Quite a lot of which was covering his torso. He had been the man behind me, shot and then knifed for good measure by Bannock.

Puzzled, I looked over at Bannock and asked, 'What does this mean?'

'Comanchero.'

I stared blankly at him. 'I have absolutely no idea what you're talking about.'

'If I'm right, this bastard hails from

south of the border. The New Mexicans were the only people down there to resist the Comanche strongly enough to force them into a permanent truce. That was decades ago, and it still holds good. Because of that they have built up a trading network with them. These traders are the only outsiders welcome in Comancheria, the Comanche homelands. And because of that they have certain influence there, and are known as Comancheros. He's one of them, sure as shooting.'

I was lost. 'I still don't understand the significance of his presence here.'

'Comancheros are traders, not warriors. Why would this piece of trash risk his life on a raid, unless it was to see a job done? Comanches don't press home their attacks. It's one of their weaknesses. They swoop in on horseback like the hounds of hell, but if they meet unexpected resistance and take casualties they move on. They never dismount and besiege an enemy.'

Bannock spat a stream of phlegm on

to the prone man, disturbing a cloud of flies, and then continued speaking. 'This scum had enough power to overturn that. He'd promised them an awful lot of something to see you dead!'

'And yet the one who did die was my guide, Mr LeMay,' I said with genuine regret. Bannock was visibly shaken. 'What, you had old Buford with you?'

'Yes,' I replied. 'He was killed on the first rush. He's lying over there.'

So saying I indicated the area where I had first been set upon. My companion rushed over to LeMay's corpse. As I joined him I was startled to see tears welling up in his eyes.

'I've known this man since I was a skinny runt. He was a true friend to me.'

Embarrassed by this sudden display of emotion I looked away and down at his friend. What I saw sickened me to the core. I had expected to see an ugly wound in the throat, made by a Comanche arrow, but nothing more. The arrow had been dragged back out, leaving a torn gaping hole, which had been filled with his own genitalia. His eyes had been gouged out, using some implement, and his fingers cut off. All over his body were deep knife cuts, where lumps of flesh had been removed. I had witnessed incidents of torture during my service in Afghanistan, but never anything like this.

'Of course,' I murmured. That explained the scuffling noises behind me the previous night. The Comanches had taken the opportunity to distract me by defiling Buford's body. I turned back to Bannock, and despite his obvious distress had to ask the question.

'I understand them wanting to confuse me, but why such savagery? It makes no sense.'

His eyes flashed with anger. 'You never give up with the questions, do you? It makes no sense to you because you're a civilized man, whatever that might mean. By their reckoning the body of an enemy goes into the afterlife

34

in the same condition that they left it: sightless and sexless. They ripped the arrow out because they're valuable, and are always recovered. It made such a darn mess because they use barbed arrows for warfare. Happy now?'

Sick, from both the scene before me, and my own insensitivity to my rescuer, I returned to where his horse stood nervously pawing the ground. I searched the desolate landscape, wondering what had unsettled the animal. Other than the carrion birds, waiting impatiently some little distance away, all was still. Bannock slowly trudged towards me, grief etched into his features, and reluctantly I enquired,

'Do we bury your friend?'

Regarding me through misty eyes he said sadly but resolutely, 'Anybody returning here would learn there was a survivor to do the digging. He stays where he lies.'

3

For the remainder of that day my new companion said little. Having only one horse between us we had to take turn and turn about riding and walking, to avoid over-tiring it. Austin was just over 200 miles of open country from Galveston, and I had travelled less than half of that before the attack. Bannock was quite obviously under orders to see me safely to President Houston at his seat of office, but I couldn't help but feel that there was more to his timely appearance.

As usual I was boiling over with questions, but by reminding myself that I wasn't dealing with a subordinate, I managed to exercise restraint. That night, however, cold-camped and wrapped in a blanket, I could contain myself no longer.

'I realize that my presence is probably

an unwanted intrusion to you, but I am in your country under orders from my government, and as such have no choice in the matter. These are new and unusual circumstances for me, and give rise to many questions. So I would be grateful if you would indulge me.'

Although we were cloaked in gloom, I was sure I detected the flash of a smile, and his response surprised me.

'Anybody who can put together that many four-dollar words deserves some answers. Ask away.'

I needed no further encouragement. 'Why, if travel is so dangerous in this country, does the president have his seat of government so far from the coast?'

'It wasn't his doing. General Lamar found the place when he was on a hunting trip. He reckoned he needed to set an example to all us Texicans. Rather than clinging to the coast, fearful of marauding Mexicans and savages and such, he wants us to settle the country. As he was president at the time, he chose for his seat, as you call it, a place on a bend of the Colorado River, for all to admire. The building work was so advanced when old Sam took over again, that he just had to live with it. Mind you, he looks more favourable on Indians than do most folks out here. Probably because he lived with the Cherokees for a while, so he maybe reckons he's not in any danger. He certainly doesn't seem afeared of them.'

I was surprised when he laughed quietly. 'Mind you, he's had to hightail it once or twice when the exalted cabinet looked like getting shot at.'

'And what is your position or occupation?' I asked.

Now that did make him laugh. 'Occupation? Ha! You come out with some absolute doosies. You lobsters must get some kind of schooling back in England.'

I bristled at being referred to as a lobster. That term came about due to the wearing of red uniforms and overly tight neck stocks, and was decidedly derogatory. 'I am a major in the British Army, and I resent that description.'

'Well pardon me all to hell, *Major*. But the British Army means nothing to me. Out here respect is given to those who've earned it.'

I clenched my teeth and pressed on. There was little benefit to be gained in falling out with the one man who knew where we were. So I tried again. 'You apparently work for the President in some capacity. You obviously know what I am, and it is only fair and proper that you should introduce yourself. We could be killed tomorrow, and then I would never find out.'

'You're a cheery one and no mistake. But you're right, we are in this together and I'll allow that you should know who you're travellin' with. I'm a volunteer ranger. I learned my trade under Captain Ben McCulloch out of San Antonio.'

'The Alamo?'

'The very same. Anywise, he and I had a falling-out, and I moved north to

Austin and sort of fell in with Sam.'

His laid-back approach to hierarchy astounded me. 'How can you just 'fall in' with a president?'

He laughed. It was quiet, as it had to be in Indian territory, but genuine. 'You've got to understand that the Republic is mighty young. Few people, spread over a lot of territory. Everybody has to pull together if we're to survive. Sam might be president but he is still just a man. A darned big one mind, and very capable.'

'Buford told me that he was a giant of six feet six inches, and that he could hammer nails into planking with his bare hands. I presume that was exaggeration to entertain a visitor.'

'Old Buf was always one for tall tales, but most stories have some truth in them. Sam is six foot something, and could certainly hammer the both of us. Mind you, he'd have to catch me first, the old buzzard.'

'Do you know why I am here to meet him?' I asked.

'Because the bloody British Empire never got over losing the thirteen colonies, and wants us to make up for it.'

He eased himself closer to me, using his elbows as leverage, so that I was able to see his eyes despite the gloom. 'Do you really believe that having thrown out the butchering Mexicans we'd swap their tyranny for a British version?'

I took all this in under his careful scrutiny. What he said certainly gave me pause. I had presumed that at least some of the population of that fledgling country might welcome our help. If this ranger's view was representative of the rest of the people, then I was here on a fool's errand. Instead of pursuing that notion, however, I changed tack.

'Your fluency of speech puzzles me. When you choose to, you talk like an educated man, yet your appearance and behaviour belies that.'

Surprisingly he did not take offence, but replied, 'I have not always been a hunter and killer of men like you.'

I made to protest but he stopped me.

41

'Nay, nay. Don't looked so shocked. You can dress up a soldier however you want, even cover him in chicken guts, but when it comes down to it his job is to kill. My ma was a schoolteacher back in Kentucky, and was determined that I should read, write and know my scriptures. That does make some folks suspicious of me.'

'You are a man of surprises, Mr Bannock, and I may well regret this, but why chicken guts?'

'Just plain Bannock will answer,' he said, rolling on to his back and settling on to the hard ground, before glancing up at me. 'Gold braid on the cuffs. Now, enough talk for tonight. We need sleep ready for tomorrow's trek.'

With that he closed his eyes and fell silent. For me sleep would not come immediately. I lay there looking up at the stars. What the ranger had said about the British troubled me. The same thought kept reverberating in my mind: *Is this mission genuine, or am I a mere pawn in a much bigger game?*

The new day dawned warm and humid. I shrugged off my blanket and staggered to my feet. Unsurprisingly Bannock was already up and about. I took a swig of tepid water and followed this with a bite of jerky. How I longed to start a fire and cook some proper food. Life in the field with my company had been luxurious compared to this. I'd even had a servant, for God's sake!

My companion was watching me with a smile on his face. 'I think you're starting to miss your regular vittles, aren't you?'

Peevishly I shook the smoked meat at him. 'How can any man exist on this?'

His reply was characteristically blunt. 'So light a fire and wait for the shindig to start.'

There was no answer to that and he knew it. To take my mind off my empty belly, I changed the subject.

'How much further do you think we have to travel?'

'Around eighty miles. At our pace say four days.' He looked at me appraisingly. 'Reckon you can take that?'

My answer was swift and most definite. 'Not on jerky and water, I can't.'

'Then it's a good job there's a homestead about fifteen miles from here. With the wealth of the British Empire behind you, you can stand me some vittles.'

'I thought you said you didn't need us out here, Mr Bannock.'

'I don't. I'm just panderin' to your cravin's. And drop the 'mister'. I'm not some kind of politico.'

'I am constantly amazed by your command of the English language.'

'You don't have to be uneducated to live on the frontier. Look at old Davy Crockett. He could put together the finest of speeches. Why do you think so many died with him at the Alamo?' So saying he mounted his horse and headed off slowly into the trackless waste.

* * *

With the sun on our backs, and climbing ever higher in the sky I wondered how long I could keep this up. How could people live in a country like this with the ever-present danger of attack? The hours passed and I trudged along, cursing the demise of my horse. I could feel a blister developing on my left foot, and knew that I should stop and nurse it, but the sight of Bannock above and to my right stopped me. He was permanently searching the horizon, and never complained. He appeared to have been born to the life, whereas I had become a soldier because it was expected of the younger of two brothers. Which was why I was plodding across the empty expanse of Texas. Or rather, limping.

By God, my foot was sore. Whether Bannock liked it or not I would have to stop and tend it or end up a cripple. I halted, intending to call up to him, but he had already stopped. His body was rigid and he was staring fixedly ahead, as though trying to see through stone. I called up to him irritably.

'What's wrong, what can you see?'

He didn't even favour me with a response. The bloody man was ignoring me. Then his left arm shot out dramatically as though he were an actor on the stage. '*Listen*! What can you hear?'

I followed his gaze, then closed my eyes and listened intently. Nothing. Nothing at all. Then I heard it. Very faintly, a cry, or maybe a scream. It was so hard to tell. Had I imagined it? Opening my eyes, I looked up at Bannock. Without turning he asked, 'Well, did you hear it?'

'I heard something, but I'm not sure what.'

Then we both heard the muffled crack of a rifle, and all doubts were gone. Bannock twisted in the saddle and shouted, 'Double up behind me. *Quickly!* That's from the Fetterman place. There must be trouble.'

All thoughts of my blister were banished. Scrambling up behind him, saddle-bags over my shoulder, I clung on for dear life as we set off at the gallop. The horse was massively over-burdened with men and iron, and I said as much.

Urging the horse to greater speed, he unbooted his rifle and bellowed back, 'He can last a few hundred yards. This is no time for caution.'

Perched uncomfortably behind the saddle, my left arm around Bannock's waist, we charged up a gentle rise towards the brow of a hill. After plodding along in each other's foot-steps for two days this was actually exhilarating. Just short of the summit he reined in viciously, threw his right leg up and over, and slid off the horse in one fluid movement. Dismounting, I followed him as he ran doubled over for the last few yards, before throwing himself down flat. I crawled crablike up to join him. As I drew level another shot rang out, only much louder now. The sight that greeted me was astonishing.

Before me was a relatively steep slope, which tapered out near a small river, presumably a tributary of the mighty Colorado. There were numerous trees dotted along both banks. Beyond this a small rough-hewn log house had been constructed. A nearby corral contained four horses. What should have been a scene of rural tranquillity had descended into a living nightmare. Nigh on a score of howling savages were twisting and weaving with astonishing speed around the farmhouse, loosing off arrows at the front windows. Their skill was truly astounding. They controlled their ponies with their legs alone, leaving both hands free to loose arrow after arrow. A man and his young son had been caught in the open, and lay skewered side by side in front of the house. Whoever was left inside knew how to shoot, though. A riderless pony continued to gallop around in concert with the others.

With a feverish intensity Bannock

grabbed my arm. 'We don't have much time. They'll fire the house to burn out whoever is left in there, an' then drive off the hosses.'

My mind reeled. 'But what can we do against so many?'

'You did all right before,' he answered.

'I didn't have any choice then. They attacked me.'

His reply stunned me, 'Yeah, well now *you*'re going to attack them!'

The full impact of what he'd just said hit me. My jaw dropped, and only one word came to mind. '*What*?'

'You're going to climb on my horse, and charge down there with that side-arm of yours. You'll need to ride right up to them, and shoot them down, face to face. I'll support you from up here. We can't let the bastards realize how few we are, or all is lost.' Tightening his grip on my arm he almost shouted, 'Do you comprehend?'

Oh, I *comprehended* all right! I was horrified. Fear was like a knife in my guts, and I could feel my bowels loosening.

'When they see that I'm alone they will surely cut me down.'

'Not if they take some losses. I know the Comanche. If they think their magic is bad they'll cut and run. But we have to move, *now!*' There was a desperate urgency in his voice. 'Trust me,' he pleaded. His earnest entreaty was supported by another shot from the house. I really didn't have any option. After all, *this was my chosen profession.*

My mind made up, I nodded, rolled over and ran down to his waiting horse. I heaved myself into the saddle, pulled the Colt out of my belt and cocked the hammer. My heart was pounding. This was sheer madness. Gripping the reins with my left hand, I rammed my heels into the horse's flanks and we were off. As we careered past Bannock and down the slope he bellowed after me, 'Powder-burn them, Thomas!'

The incline gave us a tremendous burst of speed, and I could feel a heady mix of fear and excitement surge through me. Then the ground levelled out, and we splashed through the shallow water, as yet unnoticed by the heathen devils. The trees provided cover of sorts, and I began to feel my confidence growing. As we raced up to the circling Comanches my blood was well and truly up, and I howled out a challenge. A shot rang out from the summit, and one of them was flung from his pony like a rag doll. Half a dozen of them wheeled to face me, astonishment showing on their hideously painted faces.

Galloping into their midst, I fired straight into a pair of staring eyes. The revolver bucked in my hand, and the face disappeared. Our impetus carried us through the group and I wheeled to the left, cocked and fired again. The ball struck a shrieking savage between the shoulder blades, and he collapsed sideways off his pony. Powder smoke wreathed over our group and all was mayhem. I was terribly aware that I had to maintain the pressure before they realized just how small my army was.

From the ridge I could hear Bannock shouting out, 'Follow me!' and, 'Cut them down!' to his imaginary followers. He fired again. A pony whinnied and stumbled, throwing its rider.

Spurring forward in a frenzy of blood lust, I came up behind another Indian who was on the point of loosing off an arrow at the house. I fired point blank into the back of his head. The lead ball emerged through his face, carrying gristle and brain matter with it. So close was I that his hair was smouldering from the burning powder. Then I was past him and careering on to the next. With only two chambers left I had to make them count. My onward rush was carrying me round the side of the house furthest from the ridge. The Comanches there had not witnessed my sudden assault, but had heard the rapid shooting, and were wheeling their mounts to investigate.

I charged straight for them, slamming

into one of the ponies like one ship ramming another. As its rider was jolted off I fired into the torso of another. I failed to see the result of that shot, as I was abruptly flung from the saddle, over the head of my mount, to crash down on the hard-packed earth. With all the wind smashed out of me I lay, as in a dream, completely unable to move. There was a ringing in my ears. I could taste blood in my mouth. Surely my back must be broken. Shaking my head in an attempt to clear my vision I looked up, and saw a Comanche astride his pony swiftly string an arrow. He took aim directly at me, but all I could do was watch and wait, helpless as a baby.

There belched forth a massive explosion from the house, and the Indian was blown to shreds in front of my eyes. His pony, also hit by the awesome barrage, screamed and raced off. Sucking air into my lungs I struggled to sit up, vaguely aware that bits of flesh were sticking to my face and jacket. Slowly my lungs began to fill, and with that sensation returned. Looking around me I fully expected to face new threats, but to my immense relief all I could see was dust as the Comanches fled the scene.

Bannock had been correct: they would not stand and fight if things appeared to be going against them. I drew a deep breath, heaved myself to my feet and staggered round to the front of the house. The ranger had waded across the river, and was striding purposefully towards the savage whom I had collided with. The Indian appeared to have a broken leg, and was desperately trying to drag himself towards the corralled horses. Although in terrible pain, and knowing what was to come, he nevertheless continued the struggle.

'Now that is a brave man,' I thought, watching the inevitable outcome.

Bannock narrowed the distance to two yards, then emptied his pistol into the back of the Comanche's head. The heavy ball ended his life instantly, fresh blood splashing on to the earth. My companion pivoted round with a look of satisfaction on his face, and on seeing me gave a huge and genuine smile.

'That was truly a sight to behold, Major. Jack Hays himself couldn't have done better.' Moving closer he reached out and shook my hand.

I returned the firm grip and queried, 'Who is Jack Hays?'

'I'll tell you later. Meantime your life has just been saved for the second time on this trip, and you've got her to thank for it.'

So saying he nodded back towards the house. I turned and watched as a tall, slim woman walked slowly through the door of the farmhouse. She was carrying a blunderbuss of immense proportions, and I immediately understood what had so completely destroyed my assailant. My first thought was gratitude towards her and I moved to thank her, oblivious of all the carnage around me. Getting closer, I smiled and made to speak, but the expression on her face stopped me in my tracks. Grief had transformed her features into a horrific grimace. Drifting, as in a trance, up to the bodies of her husband and son, she collapsed in front of them, sobbing and moaning. They lay lifeless, barbed war arrows protruding from their bodies. Transfixed, I didn't know what to do. From behind me Bannock placed a hand on my arm, and gently led me away.

'You can't do nothing for her in a conniption fit. Let her cry it out.'

Looking at him closely I said, 'You talk as if you have seen this sort of thing before.'

He nodded sadly. 'Many a time, and it never gets any easier. Those bastards live and breathe for this kind of sport.' He gestured towards his horse. 'We paid a price for your heroics. I'm very much afraid that old Copper's done for. Front legs broke by the looks of it.' His eyes had misted over, and I saw real pain in them.

'That's the first time I've heard you mention your horse by name,' I remarked softly.

His response chilled me. 'It doesn't pay to get too attached to anything in this country. If you stick around you'll discover that.'

Copper had obviously stumbled over the horse with which we had collided in that mad charge and was now lying, in great pain, unable to rise. I knew I had no choice. 'I'll do it,' I said gently.

Bannock just nodded and turned away. Having recovered my revolver, I stood before his crippled horse. Sighing, I pulled back the hammer. One chamber remained, as I well knew, but what a pity to have to use it like that. I took aim and then hesitated. Standing there, finger hovering over the trigger, I could hear the woman sobbing over her slaughtered family. All around me lay dead bodies. Bits of flesh were still clinging to my clothes. What kind of country was this, where hatred and violence appeared to be a way of life?

There was indeed blood on the land. Taking a deep breath, I closed my eyes and squeezed the trigger.

4

We spent that night in the farmhouse, and made a grim trio indeed. Bannock's elation at our driving off the Comanches had subsided in the face of the woman's grief. Her husband and son had died horribly in front of her eyes. She was inconsolable, and ignored all our offers of assistance. We attempted to bury them, but received an incomprehensible tirade for our trouble. So in the end we left her mewling in the dirt, and went about our business.

Bannock satisfied me that the Comanches, having been run off with heavy losses, were unlikely to return, so we collected our belongings from the ridge. He built a fire in the house, while I went over to the river to wash. Upon my return I noticed Bannock taking a curious pleasure in using the Indian's arrows as kindling for the fire. When asked about this he replied, with his usual logic, 'Comanches put a lot of time an' effort into makin' these.'

Searching around in the house produced very little that was edible. It was obvious that this family had only just been surviving. Roots and corn would go in the pot, but would not sate our hunger. Bannock reached for his knife and stepped purposefully outside. He returned with a large haunch of fresh, bloody meat. Knowing all too well where it was from, I made no comment.

For some time I had to endure the tempting smell of roasting meat, which made me realize just how hungry I was. Before eating my own, I placed a plate of food next to the woman. Wordlessly she accepted it, and started to chew. However strong the grieving process was, she had not lost the survival instinct. Observing her while she ate, I wondered what she could possibly do alone in this fearsome country.

As if reading my thoughts Bannock remarked, 'When we pull out tomorrow she'll have to come to Austin with us. Since we'll be riding her string she won't have a lot of choice.'

I looked at him askance. 'But how will she live? What will she do?'

He shrugged. 'The livery'll buy her mounts, so she'll have some coin. After that it's up to her. There's no shortage of unattached men in this country.'

★ ★ ★

As dark came on I selected one of the three wood-frame beds for myself. Stretching out, I lay there with my eyes closed. I was tired and still aching from my fall, but sleep eluded me so I put yet another question.

'Why do the Comanches persist in these awful depredations? It goes far beyond mere survival.'

Bannock thought for a while before answering. 'It's their way of life. They were here before us. They forced the

Apaches out, and reckon we're out to do the same to them. And they're probably right. There's been a sight too much hatred built up over the years, and there ain't no forgetting.'

With that he went quiet and, sure in the knowledge that the Comanches would not return, appeared to drift off to sleep. The only noise was the low keening of the woman outside. I tried to push her from my mind but it was futile. What kind of life awaited her? Her family had been butchered in front of her eyes. All her hopes and dreams of building a home with them were shattered. It made my task as an agent of empire seem somehow so trivial.

* * *

I awoke with a start. Where was the woman? I rolled over and saw Bannock regarding me grimly from the doorway. 'If she wants her kin burying we'd better get on with it, before they start getting ripe.'

61

I got to my feet. 'I'll go and talk to her,' I said.

'Kind of figured you might,' he replied drily.

I brushed past him and strode out of the house, over to where the woman had passed the night. As I approached she looked up, regarding me calmly.

'Time to leave, ain't it?' She shrugged off the blanket and stood up before me. It was then that I took my first real look at Sarah Fetterman. Tall, slim, with a gorgeous mane of raven hair, she did not look strong enough for the relentless toil of a homesteader's wife. Her face was well proportioned, and tanned from working outdoors. But it was her eyes that really held my attention. They were a piercing green. Looking into them I knew immediately that this woman was capable of surmounting any obstacle.

Spreading her arms wide she said, 'There's nothing left for me here.'

Standing there like that, in her sun-bleached cotton dress, she appeared to me a touchingly vulnerable creature. I wanted to reach out to her, but restrained myself, conscious as I was of Bannock's eyes on me.

'We can't leave them like that,' I implored. 'You must tell us where you wish them laid to rest.'

I thought she must surely break down at that, but her eerie calm held. 'I want them toted in there,' she said, indicating the farmhouse. 'And then you'll burn it to the ground!'

That brought an instant response from the ranger. 'No, that'll not answer. The smoke'll be seen for miles around.'

Her eyes moved off mine and started to blaze. 'And who might you be, mister?' There was no mistaking the challenge.

'My name is Bannock. I'm a volunteer ranger, late of Captain McCulloch's company, now working out of Austin.'

'Well, Ranger Bannock out of Austin, I'm Sarah Fetterman. This is my homestead and those are my horses. If you and your friend here don't want to walk there you'd do well and remember that.'

She half-turned and gestured at the bodies by her feet. 'This *was* my husband Joseph and my boy Josey. They were everything to me, and I won't have them buried in a shallow grave, to be dug up and picked at by critters and such. If you want to ride to Austin you'll tote them inside, and use your lucifers on my house. I *will not* leave anything for those murdering devils, and if they do return we'll be long gone. Do I make myself clear?'

I looked over at Bannock and saw defeat etched on his face.

'Mighty clear, ma'am, mighty clear,' he said. Then, resignedly looking at me, he barked out, 'Well don't just stand there, give me a hand.'

Under other circumstances I, a field officer, would not have tolerated that, but I held my peace. Together we heaved the stiffened corpses into the house. The boy, who looked about twelve, was just too pathetic. His tousled hair, now streaked with blood, was achingly poignant, and I found myself struggling to hold back tears. Bannock, apparently now recovered from his setback, had other things on his mind.

'Let's saddle the hosses and pack everything we can use before we set the place to burning. We've got to fill all the canteens. There ain't much water between here and Austin.' Before moving off he favoured me with a slight smirk. 'She might be fearsome, but she's still mighty pretty.'

For some time we attended to our tasks, until at last we were ready to depart. Bannock poured oil from the lanterns over the sparse furniture. Not wanting to waste a precious lifesaver, he blew the cooking fire into life and used the embers. As the building blazed Sarah stood watching, tears streaming down her face as she said her silent farewells.

Looking over at Bannock I cried out,

'This is horrible.'

He shrugged sadly. 'That's just the way it is out here.'

'Well, it's time it was stopped, and if your government can't manage it perhaps you need outside help.'

'You mean the goddamn British Empire,' he said scornfully. 'That'll be the day! The Comanches can be stopped. Captain Jack Hays himself proved that a few years back, and so did the New Mexicans. But there has to be the will. One of Sam Houston's faults is that he's soft on Indians. If Lamar was president things would be different and you wouldn't be standing here now.'

Despite our circumstances I was puzzled, and had to ask, 'What do you mean by that?'

'I *mean* he hates outsiders of any kind. Texas governed by the Texicans, that's his motto.'

A thought occurred to me, but now was not the time to air it. We needed to move. I turned to Sarah. Gently I asked, 'Mrs Fetterman, are you ready to go?'

She tore her anguished gaze away from the funeral pyre and replied bitterly, 'You'll call me Sarah. I'm no longer married . . . and yeah, I'm ready.'

With that we mounted up, and swung away from the raging inferno, riding off without a backward glance. To my meeting with President Houston, and whatever else awaited me in Austin.

5

It took us a further two days to ride to the capital, and thankfully they passed without incident. We rode together companionably enough, but the conversation was sparse. Sarah kept to herself and spoke little. Each night, after we had eaten, she rolled up in a blanket and appeared to sleep, but this was probably just to forestall any questions on our part. I longed to ask her more about herself, but knew that Bannock would frown on such behaviour. It was obvious that he just regarded her as a hindrance, whereas I found myself to be deeply curious about her. It was late in the afternoon of the second day, when we eventually arrived at what I supposed would be the end of my journey.

What lay before me was not at all as I had expected. Could this apparent shantytown really be the capital city of the Republic of Texas? Austin stood before me in all its glory, and I was very unimpressed. Approaching from the south-west, as we were, the wide Colorado River was off to our left, as I had expected. The many trees along its banks would provide welcome shade, and the setting was undeniably pleasant. But the city itself was just a ramshackle collection of wooden buildings of varying size and condition. There was however a noticeable street layout to them, which showed signs of planning and forethought. The main thoroughfare was wide and spacious, hinting at what the future might hold. This led up to a large mound that showed signs of surveying work.

Following my gaze Bannock said, 'Where those markers are is to be the capitol building, only they don't have the specie for it right now. The road leading up to it is named Congress Avenue. Until it gets built the cabinet meets in one of the big log shacks off to the right.'

I looked over at him and said, 'I don't know what I expected, but it wasn't this.'

'Nothing's what you expect it to be,' came an anguished voice from behind me.

I turned to Sarah in surprise. Her observations had, thus far, been few, and limited to necessities only.

'I came out here to this god-forsaken country to make a new life, and look what befell me,' she continued.

Bannock's reply was surprisingly gentle. 'It's not the land that's forsaken by God, but some of the inhabitants. Texas is my home. It has some beautiful country, but needs the heathen scum hounding out of it, to make it safe for people like you. When Lamar was president that was happening. So, Major, if you manage to gain any influence over Sam Houston, you tell him what needs doin'. Savvy?'

My reply was heartfelt. 'On that, if

nothing else, you and I are in complete agreement. And now let us water the horses and enter your capital, so I may meet my country's representative here. This journey has taken far too long already.'

Smiling, Bannock flipped me a mock salute. 'Yes sir, Major Collins. I can see I'll have to watch myself, now that we're back in civilization.'

★ ★ ★

'Bannock, you old bastard,' a voice hollered out from the edge of the settlement. 'Where've you been hiding yourself all these months?'

Spinning around and peering towards the wooden buildings, my companion shouted back, 'Give me a minute and I'll tell you.'

With surprising haste Bannock turned to me, grabbed my hand and shook it warmly. 'Never thought I'd say this to a British *soldat*, but it was a pleasure travelling with you, Major.

I'll be sure and catch up with you later, but right now I'm going to take my possibles off Mrs Fetterman's horse, and slake my thirst with a fellow ranger.'

As he collected his belongings he added, 'Don't forget what I said about Sam and the Comanches. And watch out for the politicos, they're trickier than a barrelful of rattlers.'

With that he departed leaving me feeling rather lost, and more than a little puzzled by the unseemly speed of his departure. Then I felt another, much cooler and gentler, hand in mine and I found myself looking into Sarah's eyes. Maintaining the pressure on my hand, she stared at me for what seemed like an eternity before saying,

'You're a stranger to this land, yet you saved my life, and I ain't thanked you properly before now.'

I made as if to speak.

'No, let me finish. I've been so caught up in my own grief that I've all but ignored you. That just ain't right.'

I shook my head. 'There can be no blame there, after what you've been through. Besides it was not me alone that saved you, and you did return the favour with that artillery piece of yours.'

'My recall of Ranger Bannock is that he stayed on the hill, popping *mucho* caps and hollering like a porch baby. You alone charged into the hornet's nest, and I'll be forever in your debt, Major Collins.'

I felt myself colouring, as both her gaze and her grasp held me. Not that I wanted to be released from either.

'I insist that you call me Thomas, as you would have me call you Sarah.'

'Sure enough,' she replied, only now releasing my hand. Her eyes flickered away momentarily. 'I reckon someone wants to parlee . . . Thomas.'

I turned reluctantly away, to find a small bespectacled gentleman hovering before me, clearly keen to communicate.

'I ask your pardon sir, but am I addressing Major Thomas Collins?'

I bowed slightly before answering, 'The very same, sir, and who might you be?'

Blinking slightly at my directness he replied, 'I am Charles Elliot, your contact here, and I am really most glad to see you, sir. I had expected you some days ago and feared for your safety.'

'With good reason, Mr Elliot. I was set upon by savages; both my horse and guide were killed. I only survived thanks to the intervention of a ranger called Bannock. I owe him my life.'

'As I owe you mine, Major,' interjected Sarah.

'I'm forgetting my manners, Mr Elliot,' I said hastily. 'May I introduce Sarah Fetterman to you? She joined us on our journey here.'

'You needn't be gentle on my account, Thomas.'

I had not missed her use of my given name, and my heart missed a beat as she turned to address Elliot.

'My homestead was attacked, my family slaughtered. But for the major

74

here, I too would be dead.'

Elliot was visibly shocked, 'My extreme condolences, madam. This is indeed a lawless country. It is my opinion that it requires a firm hand and much military assistance. Would you not agree, Major Collins?'

Nodding vigorously I answered, 'That will form part of my discussion with the President. I would be very grateful if you would inform him of my presence here, and ask for an interview at his earliest convenience.'

Elliot again appeared visibly shocked, 'But . . . but don't you know? Are you not aware?'

'Aware of what, man? Come, be brief, sir.'

'President Houston is not here. He and his entire cabinet are lodged in Washington . . . '

After all I had been through this was just too much.

'*Washington*! On the eastern seaboard?'

'No, no sir,' Elliot replied hurriedly,

his face colouring. 'Washington-on-the-Brazos. It is a town around one hundred miles east of here, on the Brazos River.'

I experienced mild relief, swiftly followed by a rising anger. 'But I crossed the Brazos River on my way here. By Christ, I'm even told that it's navigable by steamer!'

Sarah, obviously realizing that it was time to depart, placed a hand on my left arm and lightly squeezed it. 'You gentlemen have many things to chew over, so I'll take my leave. You must visit with me when you've more time, Major. If I can sell off some of these animals I'll take a room at the Bullock Hotel over yonder on Congress Avenue. It'll give me time to think on my future.'

Coming to my senses I said hastily, 'Don't dispose of all of your mounts. I may well have cause to buy one myself, and would much prefer to deal with you directly than with some profiteering livery man.'

In a gently teasing tone she asked, 'And do you not think that I might also wish to profit?' Then, before I could reply, she pulled on the reins and led the team of horses up towards the main street.

'A remarkable woman, sir,' commented Elliot as we watched her depart.

'That she is, Mr Elliot, that she is,' I replied. Then, recollecting my parlous situation, I turned on the unfortunate fellow and launched into a veritable tirade. 'God's blood, sir, I cannot believe that I've endured so much only to find the capital empty of all officials. Why am I here? Why are you here? Surely Ranger Bannock should have informed me? He was sent by the President to escort me here, and yet at no time did he tell me.'

Elliot looked perplexed. 'I have met a number of Rangers during my time here, but never one of that name. In whose company does he serve?'

'He told me that he had been in a

Captain McCulloch's, in San Antonio, but that he now served President Houston. As he had saved my life I took him at his word.'

Elliot's response confounded me even more. 'Washington-on-the-Brazos has served as the nation's capital since '42. I myself was informed of your coming by Albert Johnston, a former member of government. It was he who asked me to come here to greet you. I thought it strange at the time, that he of all people should know of your presence in this country, but I have always found him to be beyond reproach.'

This just got worse. 'But how did he know of my arrival in advance? And why would I be sent here if it were common knowledge that Texas was governed from elsewhere? And why the murderous assault en route? Wait a moment.' A glimmer of an idea had come to me. 'Why is the government currently in this Washington-on-the . . . ?'

'The Brazos,' came the reply. 'For

reasons of safety, mainly. It is far behind the settlement line in a more populated area, and much less exposed to marauding savages. You are only recently arrived in this country, therefore you cannot be expected to know how dire life here is. Every month there are fresh outrages by Comanche raiders. It is an atrocious state of affairs. Believe me when I say that I wish to be quit of this place at the earliest opportunity.'

The glimmer became a ray of light. 'Therefore if someone wished to assassinate me it would be far easier to achieve that end if I was sent overland to a more remote outpost.'

Elliot was aghast. 'But that could implicate someone in either of the governments. What proof can you present to support this?'

'None whatsoever. But I do know where to start. With the man who was sent to watch over me. The ranger by the name of Bannock. He departed with unseemly haste just before you arrived. Do you have any idea where I might find him?'

Elliot thought for a moment and then nodded. 'The rangers use the Treasury building as a meeting place.'

'Then that is where I must begin,'

I handed him my bags and walked slowly over to the building that he had indicated. An imposing name for a cabin of logs! I approached the left-hand section of the building and stopped.

Hesitating, I was afflicted with un-accustomed uncertainty as the thought: *Is this really a good idea?* came to me. I had no idea whom I was dealing with. Maybe I was being too impetuous. I looked back down the street: Elliot was nowhere to be seen. The man was obvi-ously no fool.

'God damn it to hell, I want some answers,' I said angrily, and definitely louder than I had intended. I pushed open the door, strode in and appraised my surroundings. The room was sur-prisingly large but gloomy, there being no lights burning and only natural illumination from the various small windows. At a table sat three men in frontier apparel. A revolver was stripped down and in pieces before them. Behind them another man lounged on a sofa in front of a window, reading some form of pamphlet. As I entered, they all looked up and inspected me keenly. I felt the intensity of their gaze, as they took in my appearance and the weapon in my belt before returning to their tasks. I cleared my throat, cursing the nerves that had all but dried me out.

'I beg you to pardon this intrusion, gentlemen, but I'm seeking a ranger by the name of Bannock. I'm informed that this is your meeting place, and that I may find him here.'

'Looks like you been misinformed, stranger. Never heard of any ranger with that handle. Sounds more like a breed of steer to me.' This from the lounger with the pamphlet.

There were guffaws all round and I felt my blood beginning to stir. I tried again.

'Ranger Bannock arrived here with me some little time ago, and was greeted by one of your number as an old friend. He himself told me that he'd been a member of Captain McCulloch's company. Surely you are not going to tell me that he too does not exist?'

One of the men at the table moved his chair, leaned back, and eyed me critically. 'For someone who just stumbled in here off the street, you're taking an awful lot on yourself, mister. You from Canada or Virginia or what?'

I decided to speak plainly. 'I am a British officer here at the invitation of your government.' That was not strictly true but it would serve. 'I am on my way to meet your president, but I would have words with Ranger Bannock first.'

'I hate the poxy British,' announced another of the three, who then spat at my feet.

I could feel the colour coming to my face. This was not going well, but I no longer cared. No one insulted my honour in such a fashion!

The man by the window had dropped the pamphlet and stood up. 'I've just told you, English, he ain't a ranger. So why don't you tote the mail while you still can?'

Still I persisted, my anger fuelling a reckless disregard for the obvious danger. 'So he's not a ranger, but you do know of him, then?'

One of the men at the table cursed under his breath and sprang to his feet. I noticed that his revolver was not the one lying in pieces.

'Tricks with words won't cut it in this company,' he spat out, his face flushed with anger.

A sudden thought occurred to me. 'What do you know of Comancheros?'

The room erupted. Another of the men still sitting at the table leapt to his feet, hurling it to one side and scattering gun parts over the floor. I reached for my weapon, as did three others in front of me. There was a deafening eruption as a gun was fired, but it came from behind me. With my hand frozen on my gun butt and my ears ringing, I backed away so that I could view the whole room. As the powder smoke cleared I saw that another man had entered the room by way of a door from the central passage. He held a smoking pistol in one hand, and was glaring at the man who had upturned the table.

'Count yourself lucky I didn't cut you down with that ball, Slade.'

He spoke in level tones, but there was no disguising the menace in his voice. Turning to face me he adopted a more conciliatory attitude. He tossed the empty pistol away into the room as though it was so much rubbish and moved towards me until we were almost nose to nose. His face was hard and craggy, with a livid scar down his left cheek. Knife or sword perhaps, maybe a duelling memento. He proffered his right hand in a crushing handshake that I only just managed to withstand.

'Name's Silas Braxton. I must apologize for the surly reception that you just received from these dogs. My men had no call to get wrathy.'

I held both his grip and his gaze whilst replying. 'May I enquire as to your position here?'

An eyelid fluttered slightly, and he gave an exaggerated sigh. 'I'm a sutler, a merchant if you will. A supplier of goods and services to the Republic. A city under construction such as this has many needs, and I attempt to satisfy them.'

I decided to push my luck again. 'So you are in a similar line of work to the Comancheros, then?'

Braxton's expression tightened as did his grip, until I thought my knuckles must break. 'Was that a statement or a question, Major Collins?'

That word really touched a nerve in this building. I side-stepped the issue by responding, 'That is for you to judge. I am newly arrived in this country, and do not know its ways as yet.'

'Then I would suggest that you learn them quickly,' Braxton replied. He maintained eye contact for a few more seconds, then released my hand and appeared to relax. 'I presume you'll be putting up at Ma Bullock's?'

'My contact, Mr Elliot, is attending to that now,' I replied.

'Oh yeah, *Mr* Elliott,' murmured Braxton. Someone in the room sniggered but their leader, for that was obviously what he was, merely nodded as he continued. 'A word of advice, Major. Be careful where you tread after dark. This is awful dangerous territory. People have been known to disappear without trace. Be warned.'

Although uttered in soothing tones the words had been loaded with menace.

'I was given to understand that the Comanche threat did not extend into the township,' I countered.

He smiled but it did not reach his eyes. 'Those witless fools are not the only dangers to be encountered in this burgh.'

Realizing that there was nothing at all to be gained by continuing the conversation I decided to take my leave. Casting my eyes over his sullen companions, I remarked, 'It was good to meet you, Mr Braxton. I look forward to renewing our acquaintance sometime.'

With that I opened the door, and walked out into the fading light of my first evening in Austin.

6

As expected, the Bullock Hotel was basic rather than opulent. What I hadn't expected was for it to smell like a sawmill. The building was a large two-storey affair with a central staircase leading up to an open-sided corridor running around the entire second floor. This provided access to all the bedrooms, and created a high ceiling, giving the lobby a spacious feel. It was constructed entirely of timber, not all of which had been fully seasoned. Its owner, Ma Bullock, was a large, jovial woman with a round sweaty face and hands like hams. In England she would have kept a tavern or a bawdy house, and very probably she knew everything about everybody. She greeted me like a long-lost friend, asking after my welfare and of my journey there. Tales of murder and mayhem did nothing to dent her jollity.

'A hot tub and some good old Texas vittles is all you need to set you up, sir. Tell cook your druthers and he'll see you don't want for anything. You deserve it after saving that lovely Mrs Fetterman from those heathen savages. If they had carried her off she'd have been a ruined woman long before now! How does Sam Houston expect people to settle this country when he won't protect them? It's beyond me.'

Thankfully Elliot came to my rescue, ushering me up the uncarpeted stairs to my room. Facing out on to Congress Avenue, it was small but comfortable. The walls were unplastered but boarded out, and there was even a rug beside the bed. After my recent confrontation I felt overwhelmingly weary. All I wanted to do was sleep, but that would have to wait for a little while at least. Elliot was looking at me shrewdly, and appeared in no hurry to depart.

'I have arranged a tub for you in the bathhouse behind the hotel, Major, but I would like to know what took place in the Treasury building, if you would indulge me?'

I nodded. 'What do you know of a Silas Braxton?'

The other man's eyebrows rose in surprise. 'So, you have encountered him, have you? He is a confidant of Mirabeau Lamar, and I have to say he makes me distinctly nervous. He has various contracts to supply the Republic, but I believe his activities go beyond that.'

My interest was aroused. 'What do you mean?'

'Lamar is fiercely opposed to any kind of foreign interference in Texas. That includes annexation by the United States or intervention by Great Britain. The disruption of communications between the various countries goes a long way toward hindering diplomatic endeavours. I am of the opinion that it is not *just* Comanche warriors who are unsettling the Texas border. It could also explain the attempt on your life.'

I gazed at the diplomat whilst trying to absorb that intelligence. A hot tub and cooked food were suddenly an overwhelming requirement.

★   ★   ★

A short while later, towelled dry and dressed in freshly brushed 'duds', as my clothes had been described to me, I found myself sitting in the restaurant at the front of the hotel. It was rough and ready, lit by flickering oil lamps, but a welcome sight none the less. All the guests sat at one long wooden table, but as it was late in the evening only Elliot and I were present, and he only out of politeness, I surmised. Outside, the main thoroughfare was an inky blackness, apparently deserted.

Following my gaze my companion said, 'It is always like this. Very few women to entertain, and lurking danger keeps the men indoors drinking and playing card games. It is an unhealthy lifestyle, but well-paid construction work keeps them here.'

Turning to my companion I asked, 'What is Washington-on-the-Brazos like? And why, if I was expected, was I not met in Galveston and guided directly there?'

The abrupt arrival of our meal delayed his response. The mouth-watering smell made me realize just how ravenous I was. I attacked my food without ceremony or delay. For some minutes neither of us said a word, but eventually I came up for air.

'What on earth is this? I have never tasted the like before.'

Elliot, smiling indulgently, replied, 'I thought you might like it. It is known as Chicken Fried Steak. Only it may surprise you to learn that it contains no chicken. It is beef pounded in rye flour, seasoned with salt and pepper and cooked slowly. I am told that the idea arrived with settlers from Prussia or thereabouts.'

I was amazed. 'What on earth are European settlers doing here?'

'They are attracted by free land grants and extravagant tales circulated back East by the government. Their only hope of domesticating this country is to populate it.'

We continued eating, until at last I had to hold up my hands in mock surrender. Elliot and I sat in companionable silence, digesting the meal for some minutes before he spoke again.

'Washington is very different from this city. It is a thriving commercial centre with a balanced population. Because it is further east it is not threatened by the Comanches every full moon. As to the reason why you are here and not there . . . '

He paused and looked at me gravely before continuing: 'I believe it is a political ploy by President Houston to delay meeting you for as long as possible. He wants the United States to learn of your arrival so as to push them towards annexing his country. He believes that only then can Texas truly survive and prosper. At the same time, if you are wandering around the interior then he does not actually have to take part in any negotiations with you. However, I am certain that he would not have sanctioned your murder. He is an honourable man and besides, something that extreme would have been of little benefit to him.'

I cut in. 'Whereas someone like Lamar loathes outsiders, and would possibly not be as fastidious.'

Elliot nodded in agreement. 'It also occurs to me that if you were to be murdered the blame could be put on agents of the United States to discredit that country. However you look at it, you have landed in a hornet's nest.'

I leaned back in my chair and sighed. 'I need some air. What say you to a cigar and a brief stroll before we turn in, Charles?'

'With pleasure,' he replied. Then, after a pause he asked, 'Are you armed?'

'Of course,' I assured him. 'I have carried my revolver at all times since leaving London.'

'Then I suggest that we keep out of the light, and within sight of the hotel at all times.'

I could see that he was in deadly earnest. Proffering my cigar wallet, I removed the glass shield from the oil lamp, I leaned forward to light up, to be followed by my companion. Puffing reflectively on the cigar, I replaced the glass and looked over at the window. That apparent barrier to the outside world provided no safety at all. The cosiness of lamplight flickering on the panes of glass was purely an illusion. Recalling my conversation with Silas Braxton a disturbing idea came to me.

Thinking aloud I said, 'We've sat here, for all to see, and enjoyed a first-class meal. Next we'll be leaving the hotel through the well-lit main entrance. Wouldn't that be a perfect opportunity for Mr Braxton to finish what he may well have started?'

Elliot had stopped drawing on his cigar and was looking startled. 'You mean you believe that he was responsible for the Comanche attack on you? A white man in league with savages. I find that very hard to believe. And yet . . . ' His voice tailed off as he considered the possibilities.

A strange calmness had settled over me. Perhaps I was at last adjusting to the brutality of this country. 'If I am right and assassins are lying in wait, then I will need your support. Do you have access to a weapon?'

Reluctantly the diminutive civil servant lifted the front of his waistcoat, revealing a small-calibre pocket pistol. Seeing my eyebrows lift in surprise he said defensively, 'It is purely to guard against footpads and the like. I have never had occasion to use it!'

I chuckled. 'Right then, let us be about our business.'

* * *

We moved quietly through to the back of the building and found ourselves in the bathhouse. As was to be expected at that time of night the room was empty, so I extinguished the two oil lamps to remove any backlight. Speaking in hushed tones I said, 'Once we are outside, stand by the door and don't move. I'll go round to the front, and look for any signs of life. If there is no sign we might feel a little foolish, but there'll be no harm done.'

In response he nodded but remained silent. I knew from experience that his mouth would be very dry, and that he would be strongly regretting his involvement in our little adventure. Easing the door open I prayed that the hinges would not give us away. Our luck held and we crept out unannounced. I gently pulled the door shut. The dark swallowed us, what little moon there was being conveniently obscured by cloud. For some minutes I simply stood there, allowing my night vision to develop. Then I moved off around the side of the hotel, stepping slowly and deliberately. My senses were heightened by fear, and the building seemed absolutely huge, its bulk looming over me. As I neared the front I pressed myself against the wooden shingles and inched my way forward, feeling the roughness against my hands. At last I was there. Light from the Bullock cast a warm glow over part of the street, but did not reach me. My heart seemed to be thumping loud enough to wake the dead. I forced myself to suck the night air into my lungs, and that action induced a steadying effect. Cautiously I forced my head away from the wall and looked out on to Congress Avenue. Not a soul was abroad that night. But for the occasional flickering oil lamp the city could have been deserted.

Then my whole body prickled with tension as I saw it. Across the street, parallel with the hotel entrance, there had been the very slightest movement. Someone over there was waiting to kill me! He, or very probably they, had been there some time, and were very likely getting restless, or maybe fighting the onset of cramp. For a moment longer I watched, then I retreated back to Elliot, who would surely be like a cat on hot coals after being left for so long.

That man gave a muffled squeak when I appeared before him like a wraith.

'God's bones sir,' he whispered. 'I had all but given you up as lost.'

Grabbing him by the arm I hissed in his ear. 'Now listen, Charles. I was right. A deadly trap has been laid for us, and it is you who will spring it!'

I could feel him tremble in my grasp as he started to protest. 'What? But I have no experience of — '

'Enough. We must act now before they tire of waiting. You will go around the other side of the hotel until you reach the front. There you will count to twenty, then fire your piece.'

I could see him staring at me, his eyes wide with shock, but at length he nodded and replied, 'I will do as you say.'

I could feel my blood stirring at the prospect of action. 'Good man. Now, let us cock our weapons here so as not to create alarm.'

This we did, and then I grasped Elliot firmly by the hand. 'Just in case,' I said, and smiled. 'Remember, twenty. Now go!'

More confident this time, I swiftly retraced my steps, and was soon back at the front of the hotel. Gripping the Colt tightly, I readied myself for a burst of speed and commenced counting steadily. At twelve there was a loud crack from off to my left, and a ball thwacked into the building opposite. The response was almost instantaneous. Two tremendous blasts came from across the street followed by a scream. Whoever had fired would be momentarily blinded, so I propelled myself away from the wall and ran furiously towards the source of the shots.

As I bounded under the awning of the building I made out two figures before me, both facing towards Elliot's position. I had achieved total surprise. Aiming dead centre at the nearer one, I closed my left eye and fired. There was a loud report, and the ball slammed into the assassin's back, throwing him forward on to his companion. Learning from the past, I had retained some night vision, and through the powder smoke saw the other man fall against the wall. Twisting like a cat he turned and began to raise his shotgun. I cocked the revolver, aimed it and yelled out, 'Drop it, drop it!'

'Go to hell, English,' he snarled.

Instantly I fired again. The ball smashed into his right shoulder, spinning him away from me. His fingers contracted in reaction, and the shotgun blasted its second volley into the night sky. Instinctively I dropped to the ground. It was that action that allowed him to escape. Lying flat, I emptied another chamber at the fleeing figure, but the round merely buried itself harmlessly in timber. I jumped to my feet and looked about me, gun at the ready. The surrounding buildings remained shrouded in darkness and unnaturally quiet, but no other threat was visible. Then I remembered the scream!

'Charles,' I called, 'where are you. Are you injured?'

As I ran towards his side of the hotel I could just make out a figure curled up against the wall. My heart leapt. *Please God, let him be alive.*

Before I could reach him a female voice called out from the main entrance.

'Thomas, is that you?' It was Sarah, great agitation evident in her voice.

'Yes,' I responded, peering over at her. 'Bring a light with all haste.'

She approached, carrying an oil lamp before her. I could see that she was wearing a nightgown with a long coat thrown hurriedly over it. Anxiety was etched on her face.

'As soon as I heard the ruckus I knew it was you,' she said. 'Are you hurt?'

'No, but I greatly fear that Charles is. Shine the lamp down here quickly.'

In the flickering glow we saw Elliot staring back up at us in apparent bewilderment.

Blood was seeping from a splinter wound in his right cheek. He spoke with difficulty, and was obviously in shock.

'Didn't step back far enough. It hurts. Oh God, it hurts! What's happened to me?'

Sarah spoke to him in soft and gentle tones. 'Easy, Charles, easy. It's just a flesh wound. You'll soon be set right. We'll get you into the hotel and take a look-see.'

As she said this Mrs Bullock and some of her staff stepped ponderously out of the hotel. I took advantage of the tumult to head back across the street, weapon at the ready, although in truth I did not expect any more trouble. There were too many witnesses, just as there had been at the Treasury building when Braxton had halted the onset of violence.

I stopped next to the man whom I had shot in the back, and kicked him hard in the ribs. Not a twitch. I grabbed his arm and rolled him over, leaning in closer to see his face. It was Slade, one of Silas Braxton's thugs. So now I knew for certain. At his side lay the shotgun, which I picked up. I was immediately surprised by its length. The twin barrels had been shortened by at least eighteen inches, making the spread of shot lethal at close range. With two such weapons aimed at us from across the street, Elliot and I would have been cut to pieces as we commenced our stroll. Angrily I resolved to keep it for my own use.

Patting down Slade's corpse I recovered a powder horn and a leather pouch containing wadding and small lead balls. In his pockets I also found a quantity of percussion caps.

Elliot was being carried, over his protests, back into the hotel. Sarah, standing radiantly in the light of the entrance, called out to me.

'Please come in now. I can't imagine what you were thinking, going out on the street after dark.'

'Apparently it was expected of me,' I replied wryly. 'You must remember that I am a foreigner, with no sense of danger.'

'Just no sense more like,' she replied, with a beguiling smile.

Together we walked back into the hotel and on up the stairs. Surprisingly she steered me towards her room.

'Your friend needs care and you need molly-grubbing. That means rest, you poor fool,' she added quickly, seeing my confused expression. 'What in the Sam Hill were you up to out there anyway? You could've been killed!'

Her face was flushed and vibrant, and she looked simply ravishing. Forgetting myself, I said as much and then waited for the inevitable slap. But it didn't come. She just stood there motionless, her hypnotic eyes fixed on mine. How long we would have remained like that I could not tell, but a groan from Elliot brought us back to reality. Sarah, gesturing towards the bed, remarked, 'I reckon your friend needs me more than you do right now.'

The time had come for some makeshift surgery. Sarah removed her coat, and rolled up the sleeves of her nightgown. Looking pointedly at me she said, 'I've got to pull out that splinter if he's to heal. It'll pain him, so you'll have to hold him down. D'you understand?'

Having been brought up to expect subservience in women, that was just too much.

'As a soldier I have seen much death and suffering. I do not need instruction from you, *madam*!'

To my chagrin she laughed and shot back, 'As a soldier you've probably caused most of it, *Major*!'

Touché, I thought with reluctant

admiration. The lady was quite something.

Putting my arms firmly on Elliot's shoulders I pressed down gently, awaiting the inevitable struggle. Sarah placed the flickering oil lamp as close to him as possible and took a deep breath. She grasped the splinter between thumb and forefinger, testing its resistance. The reaction was immediate. The little man howled with pain and struggled in my grasp.

Sarah looked at me and shrugged her shoulders. 'It's caught like a barb. It'll need pulling out from inside of his mouth.'

I grimaced and asked, 'Can you manage it?'

Reaching for the whiskey, she said firmly, 'There's no choice. If it stays in greenrod'll set in, and he'll be dead as a wagon tyre.'

She unstopped the bottle, took a large swig and then proffered it to me. 'Get some of this bark juice down him. It'll take the edge off the pain.'

Bridling at her assumption of command I commented, 'You really like to give instructions, don't you?'

She shuddered as the strong liquor hit her stomach, but managed to reply, 'Some folks take to it more than others.'

The strong drink stiffened Sarah's resolve, and without hesitation she slipped her finger and thumb into his mouth. Gripping the jagged splinter Sarah pulled steadily and relentlessly. The reaction was instantaneous. The little man screamed out as his cheek was tugged inwards. He bucked and writhed beneath me. It was all I could do to hold him. The noise ceased abruptly as he gagged on his own blood.

'For Christ's sake, hurry,' I cried out. 'He's choking!'

With a triumphant cry she whipped the bloodied object from between his teeth. 'Got it! I'd make a good sawbones.'

Swiftly I rolled Elliot on to his side so

that he could cough the blood up on to a towel.

Sarah stated calmly, 'Unless greenrod takes hold he should be fit as a fiddle before long. He'll have to stay here tonight, though, 'til the bleeding stops. I will watch over him.'

'Then he is a lucky man,' I blurted out. 'And I envy him his wound.'

'Why, Major, are you always so blunt of speech?'

'I don't know. I have never met anyone like you before.'

She looked bemused. 'I'm a widow, with little money and no prospects. Why should you be interested in the likes of me?'

I grasped her arms and pulled her closer. She did not resist and I grew bolder. 'To my eyes you look beautiful, and you say what you feel. Where I come from that is very unusual.'

'But Thomas, you hardly know me.'

'I've seen enough to want to know everything about you.'

On impulse I cradled her head in my

hand and kissed her, prepared to retreat if necessary. She stiffened slightly, then relaxed and returned the pressure. Her lips were soft, and damp with sweat after struggling with her patient. I held her tight and wallowed in the blissful moment. How long we stood like that I do not know, until a groaning from the bed pulled us back to reality. Sarah, face flushed and eyes sparkling, struggled free and gestured towards Elliot.

'He needs watching and you need sleep.'

Gazing at Elliot, who was sweating heavily on the bed, I could not dispute that, but hated leaving her nonetheless. I collected my newly acquired shotgun and made unwillingly for the door. 'Are you sure you can manage nursing him alone?'

Her eyes locked on to mine. 'I've tended worse wounds than his in my time. Now go!'

She smiled and gently touched my arm to soften the abrupt dismissal.

Reluctantly I murmured goodnight and walked along the open-sided corridor back to my room, conscious all the time of Mrs Bullock's gimlet eyes scrutinizing me from the ground floor. Feigning unawareness I went inside, closed the door, and rammed a chair up against the latch to slow down any intruders. I pulled my boots off, placed my revolver under the pillow, and sank back on to the soft bed, gratefully closing my eyes on the world. Sleep came almost immediately, delayed only by incoherent carnal thoughts that I really should have been ashamed of.

7

My eyes flicked open and I found myself staring at a wooden ceiling. Light was streaming into the room, and for a few seconds I had no idea at all where I was. Then everything came flooding back in a rush: Charles Elliot lying on the bed, bloodied and in shock, after being involved in his first gunfight. *And* Sarah, looking tired but at the same time radiant. That thought was inevitably followed by nagging doubts.

How could I allow myself an attraction to a woman I knew almost nothing about, and whose family had been slaughtered less than a week before? It was madness. I was here on behalf of the British Government to negotiate with the President of the Republic, but I was allowing myself to get distracted by an unnecessary personal involvement with a woman of dubious status. And yet how could I have pursued any other course? I appeared to be well and truly smitten. As for my mission, although I had been expressly warned to expect danger, I could not shake off the feeling that something was badly amiss with the whole venture.

I got slowly to my feet and wandered over to the basin by the window. I poured a little water into it, splashed my face, washed my hands and immediately felt refreshed. Guiltily I thought of how Sarah's night must have been, and I resolved to see her at once. I pulled the chair away from the door, then stopped. I returned to my bed and recovered both revolver and shotgun. I was obviously a marked man, so from now on they would accompany me everywhere.

I tapped gently on her bedroom door and waited hesitantly, suddenly unsure. Was I intruding? Should I return later? Then it opened, Sarah ushered me in, and all my doubts left me. She looked tired but composed, and absolutely captivating. Her patient was sound asleep, snoring gently. His pallor looked much improved and the bleeding had stopped.

Turning to Sarah I said, 'You would make an excellent physician. I don't know how you managed to settle him down last night.'

She gave a weary smile and brushed a stray hair away from her face before replying.

'A strong measure of laudanum will quiet most suffering. After you left I managed to beg a draught from Ma Bullock.'

I shook my head and laughed. 'You're amazing. I hope you'll be available if I ever get shot.'

She took an involuntary step towards me, alarm registering in her eyes. 'Don't go saying fool things like that. You seem to attract trouble like bees to honey as it is.'

For a moment we stood there,

regarding each other. Then abruptly she changed the mood. 'Are you going to tote that piece of iron around with you everywhere?'

I hefted the shotgun as I replied. 'You know what occurred last night. I seem to have made enemies, and until the issue is settled this stays with me.'

She sighed. 'I understand. I just don't want to see you bleeding, that's all. I've saved you once already, remember.'

'I know you have, but I'm safer with this than without it. Now come on, enough of such talk, let us break our fast. You must be ravenous after this night's work, and Elliot will do well enough as he is.'

'You're damn right. I'm hungry as a coyote, and he looks peaceful enough.'

So saying she rinsed her hands and face, then we went downstairs together and on into the restaurant. A kitchen hand was clearing away mugs and plates from earlier risers. About to speak, I suddenly realized that I didn't have a clue what to ask for. Baffled I wondered, *What do these people eat for breakfast?* I had absolutely no idea.

Laughing at my obvious predicament, Sarah came to the rescue. 'We'll have Rio, pinto beans and some tortillas, thank you, and we're both sharp set.'

The man responded with, 'Sure enough, ma'am,' and departed for the kitchen.

'Thank you,' I said. 'I honestly didn't know what to ask for, and even now I don't know what you've ordered. Since arriving in Texas I've been sleeping in the field.'

She looked at me askance. 'Sleeping in the what?'

'Ha. That is a military term for sleeping rough. Don't forget that I'm a soldier by trade.'

Her reply surprised me. 'I wouldn't know what a soldier looks like. Out here if there's fighting to be done a man just grabs his rifle and gets to it. That's all the rangers are, Sunday soldiers volunteering. Nowhere is safe out here, so they have to be ready at any time.'

She stopped as tears came to her eyes. I knew that she was back at her homestead reliving the last moments. I took her hands in mine, squeezing them gently. We remained like that until the food arrived. Reluctantly I released her, allowing her to wipe her eyes and return to the present.

Steaming mugs of coffee were placed before us, followed by plates of beans and what looked like sleeves of folded pastry. Taking the lead, Sarah spooned some of the beans into one of these and commenced eating with her fingers. I followed suit and found them to be delicious. For some time we chomped in silence. At length, having eaten our fill, we sat companionably together, sipping the boiling hot liquid and I broached a subject that had been troubling me.

'What are your intentions? Have you any money or any other relatives?'

She regarded me keenly over the coffee mug. 'I sold two horses to those vultures down at the livery. I kept mine — and the best of the string. It's for sale if you still want it. I ain't no road agent, but I'll be expecting a goodly sum for it.'

'But of course,' I replied, inclining my head in an ostentatious display of gallantry. 'I would not seek to take unfair advantage — in any way.'

'Good, I'm right glad to hear it,' she responded, in a tone of mock severity. 'As for my intentions, I've a cousin in Washington-on-the-Brazos, who may provide a welcome of sorts. You can't ever be sure with kin.'

That intelligence was music to my ears, and overwhelmed any common-sense that I have might have laid claim to.

'Why then, you are very welcome to accompany me,' I blurted out, 'as I too must travel there. I have urgent business with your president.'

But even as I spoke, doubts assailed me. 'Then again, perhaps it would be better if we did not travel together. It is obvious that there are people who mean to obstruct my mission, using deadly force if necessary. It could only mean more danger for you.'

She placed her hand on my sleeve and replied, 'I'm not afeared of danger, and besides, have you given thought to how you'll find Washington on your lonesome? You're a stranger hereabouts and that ranger friend of yours appears to have vamoosed.'

I answered her question with a question of my own. 'Have you heard of a man called Silas Braxton?'

She curled her lip. 'Everybody has and many are afraid of him, with good cause. He has *mucho* spondulix and is close to Mirabeau Lamar.'

'Is Braxton a ranger? Because when I visited the Treasury building he was in company with a number of them.'

'No, I don't reckon he is. He's too greedy for that, but he'll know many of them. What you must realize is that most rangers are just ordinary men. They volunteer to fight the Comanche, and can leave whenever they feel like it. They even choose their own captains. I think in your army it'll not be like that.'

'So many things about this country are different from mine.'

Sarah nodded reflectively, then appeared to come to a decision. 'I should take a look-see at my patient. When are you fixing that we leave for Washington?'

We! My heart leapt with excitement. So it was settled. We were to travel together. Excellent though that news was it did create a problem.

'My business there is urgent, but we can't both leave until Elliot can look after himself. We will need to remain here for at least one more night. By then he should be awake, and at least taking liquid.'

'Can't argue with that,' she replied, getting to her feet.

'What I want you to do then is go to my room and sleep. I have things to attend to and will not need it today, and you really need to rest.'

She looked at me intently. 'Thank

you, but keep out of trouble, I beg you, and see to the horses. Remember, we ain't agreed a price yet.'

'But of course, ma'am,' I replied, bending to kiss her hand with mock gallantry.

She laughed, and her face seemed to light up. 'Are all you British like this?'

'Only the courageous young officers,' I replied with a wink.

Still laughing, she walked out of the room and ascended the stairs; her slim form moving with ease.

When we reach Washington I'll buy her a new dress, I decided, watching her out of sight. Upon reaching the lobby I noticed that Mrs Bullock had also been observing her movements, but I thought little of it at the time.

★ ★ ★

Feeling well fed and contented with the world, I left the hotel by the main entrance. After turning right down Congress Avenue I walked over to the livery stable, which was near the southern extremity of the city. From various parts of the wooden metropolis came sounds of sawing and hammering. Construction work was obviously a permanent feature. The stable was a solid two-storey building. After I had introduced myself as Mrs Fetterman's travelling companion I was left free to inspect the two mounts that would carry us to Washington-on-the-Brazos. Both were bays of some fifteen hands, appearing healthy and up to the task. One had carried Bannock to Austin, the other had carried Sarah.

Satisfied with her choice, I left the stable and was immediately attracted by the sun glistening off the Colorado. Drifting down towards the river, I felt relatively carefree, as if the sight of water had washed away my troubles. The countryside was really quite beautiful, partially covered as it was with wild rye. I sat down on a large rock near the water's edge and allowed my mind to wander.

Inevitably Sarah was the focus of my thoughts. There was something about her that had attracted me from the moment I clapped eyes on her. I was having sexual stirrings, to be sure, but there was more to it than that. I was captivated, and in my present situation that was a bad thing indeed. I had a one-hundred-mile journey ahead of me, with any number of dangers to face, to be followed by a crucial meeting with the President of the Republic. Nevertheless it was undeniably pleasant sitting there, idly viewing the river and mulling over the delights of feminine company. Time passed, the sun moving across the sky, as I sat there in a world of my own.

Then my wandering thoughts touched on Charles Elliot, and guilt dragged me out of my idle reverie. The morning was well advanced. If Sarah was asleep, then I really needed to look in on him. Reluctantly, I hauled myself off the basking rock and made my way back towards the hotel.

As I approached the main entrance I suddenly recalled the expression on Braxton's face, so I began scanning the street and the buildings near by. Opposite and to the right of the Bullock was Russell's general store. That would have to be my next port of call. We'd need various supplies for our journey across country. By chance my eyes happened to flick beyond that building, further down the street to the Treasury.

What I saw there made my flesh crawl and my mouth go dry. Standing in front of the door by which I had entered on the previous day stood a man with his right arm in a sling. Even at that distance our eyes met, and I knew with complete certainty that he was the surviving assassin from the previous night's ambuscade. My stomach contracted and I gripped the shotgun ever tighter.

Then he smiled at me. I stopped dead, uncertainty gnawing at me. If he was so relaxed, then he did not feel threatened by me. Which meant that he was probably the bait for a trap of some kind. For a full minute we stood watching each other, the tension almost unbearable. Then he spoke with a clarity and coldness that chilled me to the bone. Even over the background hum of building activity there was no mistaking what he said.

'Any time, soldier boy, any time at all.'

A thought hit me like a mallet. Charles and Sarah were alone in the hotel behind me, whilst I, like an oaf, had been daydreaming down by the river.

'Christ almighty,' I bellowed.

I spun around and charged back to the hotel. From behind me came that mocking voice again. 'I'll see you soon. I'll see you soon!'

As I pounded through the lobby I caught a glimpse of Mrs Bullock staring at me in surprise. Ignoring her I charged up the stairs two, three at a time. Sarah's room was the nearer. I leapt for the door and I was about to launch myself through it when caution tugged at me. I thumbed back the hammers on the shotgun, kicked the door hard with my right foot and waited. The latch collapsed and the door swung open. Elliot was lying on the bed ... but there was something different about him. I moved carefully into the room and then saw it: a huge bruise on his forehead the size of an egg. His breathing was laboured, but at least he was still alive.

'Oh God, Sarah!'

In a frenzy, I bolted out of the room and down the corridor. All caution had left me. I threw myself into my room to be confronted by ... nothing. The bedroom was completely empty. But whereas before it showed only signs of sleep, now the bed was in total disarray. There had been a violent struggle with one clear outcome: Sarah had been taken.

8

Hands trembling with reaction, I stood by the bed and took a deep breath. I had to calm down or I could well get myself killed.

'Think man, think,' I berated myself, very aware that somebody must have seen or heard something. 'Of course,' I realized, slapping my forehead. 'Mrs Bullock!'

Having gently released the hammers down on to the percussion caps, I strode back through the door and along the corridor. Sure enough that woman was standing in the lobby staring up at me. It occurred to me that she was very quiet, considering that I had just kicked in two of her bedroom doors. Descending the stairs, I cried out, 'What happened here? What did you see?'

She swallowed but maintained her composure. 'I've no notion of what you speak, Major Collins, but I'll be expecting payment for the damage to my property.'

'Damn your property, and damn you, madam,' I barked out. 'Mrs Fetterman has been abducted under your roof and I would know who did it.'

'I saw nothing worth my time. I'm a busy woman with many responsibilities,' she replied tartly.

'And what of Charles Elliot? Who attacked him?' Getting no response, I persisted. 'He represents the British Government, and has been brutally attacked, in *your* hotel.'

That point struck home, and she wilted slightly under my verbal assault. 'I cain't be expected to know every little thing that goes on here,' she whined. 'But I'm mortal grieved for Mr Elliot. He's such a nice gentleman.'

'Well then, you'd better hope that he survives,' I snarled, abruptly turning on my heel. It was obvious to me that I was not going to obtain any help from that quarter. Rapidly ascending the stairs I made for the room where Elliot lay. I desperately needed time to think. I pushed open the door and entered the room.

The sudden pressure on my neck was devastating! I was gripped in a crushing armlock that brooked no resistance. A hand closed around my mouth, as a familiar voice whispered in my ear. 'Hello again, *Major*.'

I froze with shock.

'Keep your voice low. I don't think that hag saw me, so let's keep it that way.'

So saying Bannock abruptly released his hold, and then put out a hand to steady me as I turned to face him. Angrily I pushed it away and hissed, 'What the devil brings you back?'

'The devil's work itself, my friend,' he replied evenly.

'Friend is it now? It's very odd that Sarah disappears, Elliot is attacked and then you suddenly reappear.' Anger was building inside me as I continued, 'Who are you working for and what message do you carry?'

'I bring no message. I come to help you make sense of all this,' he answered, refusing to be provoked.

I was by this time boiling with rage. 'I don't believe you, and if I have to beat it out of you I will.'

He looked me up and down and smiled. 'You might have some fancy moves with that belt gun, but I could wup you to a frazzle.'

I just stood there clenching my fists and he sighed. 'You're just mad enough to offer it.' Clearly exasperated he tried again. 'Braxton has her. He checked this room first but only found *that*.' He indicated the unfortunate Elliot.

His words stunned me. My worst fears had been confirmed.

'But why? What possible reason would he have? He must have known he would be seen.'

'He doesn't care. Don't you understand? This is Lamar's city and he's Lamar's cur.'

I sank back into a chair. 'This is

lunacy. Why would he kidnap Sarah, and if he is so ruthless why is Elliot still alive?'

'He's a killer to be sure, but only when he sees a need. That sack of shit was no threat to him. Sarah he took because of you.'

'*Me!*' I exclaimed in amazement. Then the fog over my brain began to clear and I saw it all. 'They're using her to get to me in some way.'

Bannock silently clapped his hands. 'Bravo, Major, you're getting there,' he said mockingly. Before I could respond he continued, 'Braxton's under orders to stop you reaching Sam Houston, but you've been a mite hard to kill and he was getting desperate. Then he hears of your little romance and he gets to thinking. He *expects* you to go after the woman. Even if he doesn't slay you out there he'll have achieved his aim. If you're wandering around West Texas you're no use to the goddamned British Empire.'

This was too hard to take. After all

that Sarah had endured she was now held prisoner, to influence my actions.

'But where will he take her? He can't hold on to her for ever!' An awful thought occurred to me. 'Surely he won't kill her.'

Bannock answered in a voice that was too calm, too controlled. 'No. Even Braxton wouldn't kill a white woman in cold blood. If word got round it would create too much ill feeling. But if that woman were to be captured by Comanches and then just disappear . . . ' He shrugged and left the sentence unfinished. 'Well, who's to say? It happens all the time near the settlement line.'

I felt as though my head was about to explode. I was beside myself with anger, but there was no one to take it out on. Then it came to me. '*Bullock*. She knew. She must have been a party to it.'

I lurched for the door but Bannock blocked my path. 'Yeah, she knew, but she had no choice. When General Lamar found this place it was just a few huts by the river. He opined it would be a good place to rule his Texas empire from, so when he became President Lamar he made it happen. Everybody here owes their livelihood to him. Houston doesn't like the place, which is why he's on the Brazos. So you see, Ma Bullock didn't really have any choice.'

I felt ill. My head was throbbing.

Why had I sat by the river for so long? I raged inside, cursing myself for a damn fool. Then everything suddenly became so clear to me. There really wasn't anything to consider. I would go after Sarah and my mission could go hang. I said as much to Bannock and he gave a slow smile.

'I kind of expected you to say such.'

'And what of you? What is your position in all this? If you know so much, why did you not stop them taking her?'

'Ever since I saved your hide, all you've done is ask fool questions. I told you before. I was sent by Sam to keep an eye out for you. He couldn't give two figs for the British Empire, but he doesn't want one of its agents getting slaughtered in his country. It'd make him look sloppy! As for stopping Braxton . . . well, I was only one man. He had his bartrash with him, and you were sunning yourself down by the river.'

He had me there and he knew it. I watched him carefully and took a deep breath.

'When I go after her will you help me?'

'I thought you didn't trust me,' he replied slyly. 'You were out to trade punches with me only a few minutes ago, yet now you want me to lead you into Comancheria after a pack of murdering cut-throats. And you haven't even said *please*!'

I swallowed hard. This was not easy for me. As an officer I was used to telling rather than asking, but the situation dictated otherwise.

'I can't force you to help me and I won't beg, but you know that I can't do it alone. I don't know the country or the people. So I'm asking you: *please* help me. If only because Sarah doesn't deserve all this.'

Bannock took all that in and then nodded thoughtfully. 'Deserve's got nothing to do with it, but that was plenty hard for you, wasn't it? So I guess I'll just string along after all. Only don't point that iron at me,' he said, gesturing at my shotgun.

* * *

My innkeeper looked up apprehensively as I descended the stairs once more. It was obvious that she just wanted rid of me, and I was about to oblige.

'I intend to have a meeting with President Houston at the earliest opportunity, and I will be giving him a full report on what has taken place here!' I informed her.

I had her complete attention, which no doubt afforded Bannock the opportunity he needed to slip out at the rear of the hotel. 'While I am absent I expect you to care for my colleague, Mr Elliot. You are partly to blame for his condition, and will therefore afford him your best attention. Do I make myself clear?'

She appeared cowed, if unrepentant, and assured me that she would do as I asked. Satisfied I returned to my own room to collect my belongings. I had no idea of what lay ahead, but they had to be safer with me.

And so, less than twenty-four eventful hours after arriving in the capital, I was back in the saddle, sporting a new slouch hat and leading my supposedly spare mount eastwards.

9

For the first few hours we rode in relative silence. Having linked up beyond the city, we had soon swung west. My companion was keen to put as much distance between us, and the capital as possible. Periodically he would rein in and use my spyglass to scrutinize our backtrail.

There did not appear to be anyone following us, but this failed to give Bannock any comfort. 'You never can tell for sure. It depends how far back they hang. There's too much cover. Once we get on the plateau things'll be different.'

I loathed being unfamiliar with my surroundings. It made me feel terribly vulnerable, and I said as much to my companion. He eased up the pace to a gentle trot and began to talk. But I noticed that he never stopped scanning the horizon all around us.

'Reckon you need to know what we're up against. It's my belief that Braxton will leave two or three guns around the Balcones Escarpment. It's all rough ground with tree-covered hills as you move up to the Edwards Plateau. Make a perfect place to draw down on you. You'll never spot 'em hidden there.'

I felt disheartened, especially with all the emphasis placed on me. Surely we weren't to be frustrated so soon.

'How then do we proceed? Can we not go around behind them?'

'You're forgetting one thing. They're expecting you alone, so that's what they'll get. You'll cold camp at the foot of the escarpment tonight, while I work my way around behind them. Come first light you'll start moving up into the hills, *slowly*, mind.'

He had obviously given the situation much thought and I listened carefully, looking for any obvious flaws in his plan. The prospect of being used as bait again did not appeal.

'If we make it up to the higher ground, on to this plateau, what will we find there?'

Bannock slowed to a halt, and just sat his horse, looking at me. At length he answered.

'Then we'll truly be in a world of hurt. It's flat and dry up there, with few trees and little shade. At this time of year we'll fry during the day, but at least get some respite after sundown. In winter a man can freeze solid in the saddle. We'll be in the southern tip of Comancheria, the Comanche homelands. There no white man is welcome or safe. Braxton will have clear passage because he'll have at least one New Mexican trader with him. A Comanchero. You recall them, don't you?'

'Of course,' I exclaimed. 'When I confronted them with that name in the Treasury building they went berserk.'

'They would. Braxton's a mite touchy over that connection, because

139

every honest Texican loathes Coman-cheros. They supply the savages with weapons and tools. If we could prove that he was in deep with them he'd be finished.'

Thinking aloud I asked, 'What if that linked up his paymaster, General Lamar, to everything that's happened to me since I arrived here?'

Bannock whistled softly. 'You sorely love to tread dangerously don't you? Sam would be tickled pink with that. His main rival discredited, and even on the run.'

'We'd need both Braxton and a trader, alive and talking in Washington,' I reflected. 'That's not going to be easy, is it?' But it was an idea and I could see that the ranger was intrigued by it. He sat his horse, eyes fixed on mine, considering the possibilities.

I smiled. 'Don't forget to keep watch. We don't want anyone sneaking up on us.'

He snorted, 'That'll be the day,' but

he went back to searching the horizon anyway.

*   *   *

A couple more hours passed before the sun dropped below the horizon, signalling the end of another day. The terrain was undoubtedly getting rougher, and appeared to be rising steadily before us. Bannock motioned me to halt. Looking at me thoughtfully he said, 'This is as far as you go today. I don't think we've been spotted yet.'

We dismounted and I removed the saddle from my horse. Whilst I rubbed him down Bannock reached into his pack for biscuits and jerky. 'I'll eat with you 'til dark and then I skedaddle. You'd better hand me that glass. I'll need it come sunup.'

I passed it to him, saying, 'Have it with pleasure, but look after it. It has come a long way.'

'Like you, Major,' he said through a mouthful of beef. 'I'll bet you really missed these vittles last night.'

I groaned. *God almighty, was the chicken fried steak only last night?* Aloud I said, 'It seems an age ago. I've killed a man since then.'

'Don't let that bother you. Slade needed killing.'

Doubtfully I asked, 'Does anyone really need killing?'

His reply was unyielding. 'If you lived out here you wouldn't have to ask that. This isn't a war between countries you're involved in now. It's a fight for survival. Comanches live for the next raid, the next captive. If they get their hands on Sarah Fetterman they'll ruin her for the pleasure of it. If they don't rape her to death, they'll torture her and treat her worse than an animal. We have to get to her before Braxton sells her, or you'll never see her again. So if you come up against any of his men tomorrow keep that in mind.'

I chewed my cold supper and considered his little speech. He was right, of course. This situation couldn't be compared to anything else that I had encountered.

We sat in companionable silence until darkness fell. Then the other man grasped my hand and held it firmly.

'Remember, when it gets light move slowly on foot as if you're unsure how to proceed. If you hear shots ride like hell, because I'll need help fast. And don't forget, if you hope to see that woman again you've got to fight real mean.'

I returned the handshake warmly. 'I'll do my best. Just you be careful out there, Ranger Bannock.'

He stepped back, mounted his horse, flipped me a casual salute and moved carefully off into the blackness. Almost immediately I felt alone and a little despondent. I had grown used to his company, and now he was gone again.

After hobbling my horse I wrapped myself in my thick blanket, and lay down using the saddle as a rather hard pillow. There was nothing that I could usefully do until sunup, so I determined to get plenty of sleep that night.

I awoke stiff from the hard ground despite the thickness of the blanket. Shrugging it off I staggered to my feet. My body cried out for hot coffee, but a fire was out of the question. Shuffling from side to side I stamped my feet to get the circulation moving.

I pondered on Bannock's probable whereabouts. It occurred to me that his night must have been far more unpleasant than mine. With my back to the escarpment and looking east, I could just make out the first rays of light announcing the start of a new day. My stomach felt on edge, but I forced myself to eat two of the corndodgers purchased at Russell's store.

Having saddled my horse I tied on my blanket, and then looked up at the sky again. It was noticeably brightening, and I was now able to make out my little campsite in detail. I could just see the ground rising off to the west. It was time to move. By the time I got into the hills proper it would be full daylight, and then my ordeal would really begin. I checked the loads on both weapons, and made sure that all the percussion caps were seated properly. I had already suffered one misfire with almost lethal consequences.

Taking the reins in my left hand and the shotgun in my right, I set off at a steady pace. I intended that any observers should see that I was conserving my horse without appearing alarmed in any way. The foothills lay before me, steep and tree-covered and infinitely threatening; yet to the casual traveller all would have appeared normal. If Bannock's theory was correct I could even then be highlighted in a gunsight, with the sun directly behind me. The thought brought forth a wave of nausea, and a knife seemed to be twisting in my guts. I was sick and tired of being a target. Reluctantly I dismounted and started picking my way through the rocks and up into the trees.

'This is intolerable,' I groaned softly.

Every fibre of my body screamed out for relief from the stress. Through the sweat pouring off my forehead I strained to detect anything out of the ordinary. Every boulder, every tree, could've concealed a marksman. I felt as though I was moving in slow motion. Every step forward seemed to take an age. I stopped to take a drink. I was sweating far more than was justified by the heat. Cursing Bannock, I began to feel sorry for myself.

Resuming my steady plod up the hillside I suddenly became aware of a strange creature that had appeared a short distance away. It resembled a deer, but had two short horns in place of antlers. Before I had time to react it turned and sped off up the slope at an unbelievable pace. Despite my fraught situation I marvelled at its sheer speed. It was the fastest creature that I had ever come across. As I watched it disappear my attention was caught by a puff of smoke off to the right, followed by a sharp crack. Stupidly I wondered how anyone could contemplate hitting that fleeing animal with a rifle. Then there was a scream a mere few yards in front of me, and a man's body toppled out from behind a tree.

'*Christ!*' I shouted in alarm. Releasing my horse I dropped rapidly to the ground.

The fellow lying on the ground screamed out, 'I'm hit, Frank, I'm hit. The bastard's got me!'

From way off to my right came a frantic reply. 'It weren't English, Ty. Came from back of us.'

I lay there wondering what to do for the best. My instincts cried out for me to stay down. The wounded man had been hit in the left shoulder, but had retained his revolver. He snapped a shot off in my direction, kicking up dirt a yard or so from my position. Groaning with pain, Ty again cocked the revolver, this time taking more deliberate aim. Recalling Bannock's words, *If you hope to see that woman again you've got to fight real mean*, I rolled rapidly twice to my left and then levelled the shotgun. The revolver fired again, the ball hitting the spot I had just vacated. Swiftly sighting down the twin barrels I pulled the first trigger. There was a tremendous blast, and I winced as my shoulder absorbed the heavy recoil. From before me came a howl of agony. My hurried response had definitely got a result. Jumping up I charged towards my assailant. As I ran, I shifted the shotgun to my left hand and drew the Colt.

The man called Ty was lying on his side, blood weeping from various lacerations to his face and neck. I'd been too far away to obtain a close grouping, but a number of pellets had struck him. Blubbering with shock, but miraculously still clutching his revolver, he attempted to draw a bead on me. Without any hesitation I aimed my handgun directly at his face and pulled the trigger. At such close range the lead ball smashed in above the bridge of his nose with tremendous force. Flattened by the impact, the soft metal spread out, carrying brain and skull fragments with it as it made a bloody exit. Ty's head snapped back, and then lolled forward as his life ended.

Standing over him, I belatedly remembered the distant voice calling to him; I dropped to the ground just as a ball smacked into the tree behind which Ty had been skulking. Tiny splinters showered into the side of my face, narrowly missing my eyes. An idea came to me instantly, and I screamed out in apparent horror. 'My eyes. I can't see,' followed by, 'Sweet Jesus I'm blind, I'm blind!'

All the time wailing with pain and despair, I pulled back the other hammer on the shotgun and lay there, praying that Bannock would stand firm and keep his distance. The sound of pounding feet announced Frank's arrival. I took a quick glance through narrowed eyes. The gunman was tall, swarthy and heavy set, and his breathing sounded laboured. There was another distant rifle crack, but he was moving too fast and Bannock's ball missed. As he came to a skidding halt before me I suddenly looked up at him and winked.

Frank's expression of glee turned to horror as I squeezed off the other barrel. Held loosely in front of me the shotgun stock recoiled violently into my thigh causing me to cry out in pain, but this was drowned out by the blast as the full load caught him in the chest. He was blown back several feet and died without a sound, such was the terrible impact. His upper torso was reduced to bloody pulp.

For several seconds there was absolute silence. Then from further up the hill a voice hesitantly called out, 'Did you get the poxy prick, Frank?'

There was a further period of quiet followed by, 'Frank! Answer me. Did you get him?' This time there was a hint of hysteria evident in his voice. I pondered whether to reply or stay silent, but I was feeling vindictive and just couldn't resist. Gazing at the human wreckage in front of me I bellowed out, 'Frank can't answer you. He's not well!'

There was another stunned silence on the hillside, and I could well imagine what was going through the man's mind. Having set a lethal trap for one lone stranger everything had turned against him. I wondered how many of them were left. If Bannock was correct there might only be the one. I didn't have long to wait. Bannock's voice sounded off about twenty yards away. He'd obviously taken advantage of the action to move in closer. 'There's only the one bushwhacker left, Major. Let's take him alive; he may be useful to us.'

To me that sounded easier said than done, and I began reloading the shotgun. It was an awkward process when carried out lying down, and I was grateful to have a second pair of eyes covering me.

Bannock shouted up the hill. 'You up there. What's your handle?'

Silence!

151

He tried again. 'Come out slowly with your hands high or it'll go badly for you.'

Our answer was the crack of a rifle. 'Piss off, Beaujolais. I know your voice. You'll kill me anyhow, so no deal.'

Beaujolais, I wondered. *What on earth does that mean?*

It obviously meant something to my companion, as he began screaming obscenities up the slope. 'I know you, Jonas Ward, you little shit! When I catch up with you I'll carve my initials in your tits.'

Jonas, not knowing when to keep quiet, replied with his own brand of vitriol, so I carefully moved towards the shouting. There was plenty of cover, but as I got closer I took no chances and dropped down on to all fours. From below, Bannock continued with his vocal covering fire.

'There's a whole company of rangers down here, you little bastard, so why don't you just give up and save us all a lot of trouble?'

152

The mention of others must have reminded Jonas that he was up against at least two of us, because this time he remained silent. Lying perfectly still, I strained to catch any sound that would give away his position. All was quiet, and I realized that he was probably doing exactly the same as me: lying prone, gun at the ready waiting for the other to approach. The hillside was covered with trees, either individually or in thickets, and I knew that unless one of us made a mistake we could remain skulking in the foliage for hours.

Resolving to break the deadlock, I cocked both hammers on the shotgun, and placed it gently on the ground, facing in Jonas's general direction. I hefted a large stone in my hand, hurled it in front of me and waited for it to land. It crashed into a tree trunk some yards away. Instantly there was the loud crack of a rifle from a clump of trees just slightly higher up the hill and, more important, a puff of smoke.

Now, I urged myself, *before he reloads!*

Grabbing the shotgun I leapt to my feet, and fired both barrels at once in that direction. The brutal recoil bruised my shoulder, and the smoke completely obscured my position. With the smell of sulphur strong in my nostrils I threw the gun aside, and raced out at a right angle from my prey. Drawing my Colt I prayed that the other man would be befuddled by the blast of shot. A ninety-degree turn and I was leaping across the uneven ground. I glimpsed a figure in the trees frantically struggling to brush splinters from his face and upper torso. I had him! Catching sight of me, he desperately swung a pistol around to bring me down. My revolver was cocked and ready, so, shuddering to a halt, I took a careful two-handed aim.

Then I again recalled Bannock's words to me, *Let's take him alive,* and I hesitated. The thought occurred that he could be of use in freeing Sarah. That momentary delay almost killed me. As if in slow motion, I watched him level his long-barrelled pistol at me and realized my awful error. In the same instant there was a terrific crack from close behind me, and my opponent was sent reeling by a smashing blow to his left leg.

Spinning around I found Bannock standing mere feet behind me, wreathed in smoke from the discharge of his rifle.

'That was a damn fool thing to do,' he spat at me.

Whilst secretly agreeing with him I nevertheless countered with, 'You told me you wanted him alive.'

Shaking his head he replied, 'Yeah, but not you dead by way of exchange.' Nodding towards the agonized Jonas he continued, 'That little weasel's not worth a drop of our blood.'

'Is he the last of them?' Even as I asked this, I realized that it was a stupid question. We would hardly be conversing in the open if we were still under threat. Bannock just grunted and moved towards the highly agitated individual in front of him.

'You bastard son of a thousand whores. You shot my good leg,' howled Jonas. 'Every time I see you I get hurt. You miserable skunk!' And so it went on. Bannock appeared to be completely unaffected by it all, so I walked back down the hill to collect my shotgun.

When I returned Jonas turned his invective on me. 'You goddamned English cur. You used that scattergun on me. Look what you've done to my face. Oh Christ, Maggie'll never look at me again.'

Before I could reply Bannock kicked his wounded leg, saying as he did so, 'You were an ugly little shit before he unloaded that twelve-gauge on you, and Maggie's half-blind from the pox anyway.'

Speechless with pain and rage, all Jonas could do was scream and dribble. Looking at him properly for the first time I could see that he was indeed a pitiful specimen. Even writhing on the ground he looked short, grubby and exceptionally ugly, with very few teeth and even less hair. My shotgun had added a number of splinter wounds to his face, but I imagined that the overall picture of dissolution was little altered. Sitting down on a rock I reloaded the weapon and eased the hammers down on freshly seated caps.

Bannock, watching this, smiled. 'That's a real crowd pleaser you've got there. Remind me to keep back of you.' Gesturing at Jonas he continued, 'This undersized runt has got in my way a couple of times too often, but this'll be the last.'

Hearing this the little man abruptly stopped howling and looked up at us in sheer terror.

'You don't mean to kill me? *For what?* I never shot at you. It was the other two. Braxton made me. I was just here to carry messages, for Christ's sake.'

Bannock eyed him impassively. 'And what was the message to be? That my friend here was lying butchered on a hillside, and your knuckleheaded leader could do what he wanted with the woman.'

Snorting dismissively Jonas replied, 'The bitch is finished anyway, once the Comanches get hold of her, whatever happens here.'

Rage engulfed me. There was a tremendous throbbing behind my temples, and I felt as if my head was about to explode. Sarah was held captive by trash such as this, and he was openly mocking us. I lurched forward, shotgun clenched in both hands. Bannock threw himself in front of me and grabbed my shoulders. His eyes burned into mine.

'*Not yet!* We need answers first. Then you can finish him.' He said this softly so that our prisoner would not hear, but the authority in his voice cut through my anger and under the assault of common sense it began to dissipate.

Of course, I reasoned to myself. At

the very least this scum'll know the direction taken by Braxton and his band.

Nodding my agreement I backed off, and Bannock turned back to face Jonas.

'Right! Simple trade. Tell me what I need to know or I'll let him loose with that scattergun again. It's your choice. But just so you know, my friend here is smitten with that 'bitch' and what you just said is eating him up inside.'

My mind raced. Was I? Was I really in love with her? Yes I supposed, I must be. Why else would I abandon such an important mission, jeopardize my career *and* place myself in such peril?

Bannock's voice cut through my thoughts. 'Where's Braxton headed. How many riders has he got with him?'

Jonas's urchin-like face creased up with a show of thought. There was little intelligence there, but a definite display of deviousness.

In a whining tone he asked, 'How do I know you won't just up and shoot me anyhow once I've talked?'

159

The ranger's response to that shocked both Jonas and myself. He stepped up next to the wounded man, and brought the butt of his rifle sharply down on the shattered leg. The resultant scream was ear splitting, and despite my strong revulsion for the wretch I couldn't stop myself cringing. Bannock however remained completely impassive as he spoke again.

'How many and how far away? Tell me now or I'll use the other end and you'll never walk again.'

Jonas continued howling and snivelling, but as Bannock upended his rifle he threw his arms up in supplication and bawled out, 'All right, all right. I'll talk for pity's sake. Just let me alone.' He took a deep shuddering breath and continued. 'Silas has got four riders with him and that half-breed Mex that he keeps in tow.'

Bannock interrupted. 'You mean Huerta?'

Jonas, keen to cooperate, hastily nodded his agreement. Looking over at me Bannock explained, 'Huerta's a

Comanchero. To this piece of shit he's just a 'breed, but when they're in Comanche country he's all that'll keep them alive.'

Before he could continue I interrupted, demanding of Jonas, 'How is the woman? How are they treating her?'

The other man's eyes glittered as he licked his lips and replied, 'Two of them wanted to stake her out and use her good, but Silas wouldn't allow it.'

A red mist came down over my eyes. My mouth had gone dry and I croaked, 'Why not?'

'Because he wants his penny piece for her and didn't want damaged goods. It's all rocks with him.' Despite the debilitating pain he sniggered. 'He told them if they had to do it, to use the horses. Ha, ha. He's all heart, is Silas.'

I was starting to tremble with reaction. Seeing this, Bannock took over the questioning again. 'Last thing. Where they headed?'

'There's a band of Pehnahterkuh up near the San Saba. He fixes to doing the trade and then heading back this way to see what became of English.' Looking at us speculatively he continued, 'Reckon he's in for a shock, eh?'

'No more than you, my friend,' answered Bannock.

The reply was laden with menace, a fact not missed by Jonas. 'What is you thinkin' on, you bastard? I told you what you wanted. We agreed.'

'All I agreed was not to let our foreign visitor here use that twelve-gauge on you again.' Turning to me he said conversationally, 'Why don't you go down the hillside, and see what weapons his *compadres* were packing? If we're chasing down six desperadoes *and* the Comanche nation we'll need whatever we can get.'

I hesitated and he said more forcefully, 'It's for the best.'

Staring at him, I knew what was about to happen, but try as I might I couldn't find it in me to protest. That little snake had helped abduct Sarah and then attempted to ambush me out here in the wilds. He had used up all his luck.

Turning away I moved deliberately back down the hillside towards Frank's body. I could hear Jonas wailing and sobbing again as he pleaded for mercy. Then in desperation he began calling out to me. 'For pity's sake, English, stop him. I don't deserve this. I did nothing to you!'

There was a sharp crack and then total silence. I wondered just how many more men were going to die before my business in Texas was concluded.

10

It had been a long, gruelling climb for both man and beast, but at last we were on the plateau and there everything changed. Gone were the thickets of juniper trees and wildflowers spread across the broken hillside. As far as the eye could see, on all sides, there stretched miles of empty grazing land. The temperature had soared, and there was little or no breeze as we jogged along.

I now carried another Paterson Colt Holster Model revolver tucked into my belt. This weapon, which I had recovered from beside Ty's shattered body, had a shorter barrel but, conveniently, the same .36 bore, and crucially appeared to be in good order. I now had enviable firepower at my command. It was encouraging to think that however many desperadoes we were following, I should be able to give a good account of myself. Thoughts of Sarah began crowding in on me again, and to escape them I opened up a conversation with Bannock. As ever he was relentlessly scanning the horizon, but seemed content to talk.

'As usual I have some questions for you,' I ventured warily.

Turning in his saddle Bannock regarded me with what could almost have been affection. 'I wouldn't expect anything less.'

Responding with a genuine smile I asked, 'What on earth was that creature that I startled just before you opened fire?'

'That was a pronghorn,' he replied. 'It's the fastest thing on four legs in these parts. The only chance you have to bring one down is to catch it unawares. Like you nearly did.'

Recalling its awesome turn of speed I could only agree with him. 'And who are the Pehnahterkuh that Jonas spoke of?'

All trace of good humour left his face. 'They are the worst enemy we Texicans have got. They are a band of looting, pillaging Comanches that dominated this whole area until a few years back. When Lamar was president he went to war with them, using Jack Hays and other ranger captains to attack them. We never let up and finally broke their power. Most of what were left drifted up north, but there are bands of scavengers still roaming the plateau. To them we are known as *Tejanos*. There can never be any peace between us. It can only end when they are wiped clear off the face of the earth.'

I was watching him carefully. 'You said *we* just now. Were you a part of that war?'

'For a while,' he replied guardedly.

I was intrigued. 'Why, what happened?'

Bannock sighed. 'There's no big secret. Lamar instructed his ranger captains to kill anything that walked or crawled on the plateau. I've no problem with killing; never have had, but not women and children. I know they do it to us, but that don't make it right. So anyhow, Ben McCulloch and I had words and we parted company. When Ol' Sam became El Presidente again he asked me to come work for him.'

I understood immediately. 'So that's why you had to lie low in Austin, because of Lamar's influence.'

'You're getting the hang of it, Major. I ain't popular around his lackeys. Sam halted the Injun campaigns because they were costing us too much, and as you probably know Texas is broke. But a lot of folk on the frontier reckon that was a big mistake and they could be right.'

I had listened to everything he'd said, but I suddenly had Sarah's features in my mind.

'How far behind them are we?' I blurted out anxiously.

Bannock's swift scrutiny took in my agitation. 'If you let it get to you we're both finished, an' I ain't ready to meet my maker just yet!'

'I can't help it,' I cried out. 'I keep thinking of Sarah out there somewhere, and what could be happening to her.'

'If it helps any, I think Jonas was telling the truth for once in his miserable life. Braxton won't want her spoiled, and besides he needs to keep moving until he knows what's happened to you. You might be only one man, but you've been harder to kill than most.'

I absorbed that in silence, oblivious to the veiled compliment, before posing my next question. 'Doesn't anyone live out here? It seems hard to believe that so much land could be completely empty.'

'Soil's too poor for farming. The grazing's good but it's too dangerous for ranching so white folks stay away. Until Colt made that new shooting iron, nobody could defend the open plains. For a rifle you need cover to hunker down and reload. Out here you'll get two shots at best and then they're on you. Hays taught us that the revolver could change everything.'

'But you're not carrying one,' I teased.

'I don't need to. I've got the British Army with me,' he retorted.

'If only that were true,' I answered with feeling. 'You've mentioned this man Hays before. Who is he?'

The ranger adopted an almost reverential air as he answered. 'Captain John Coffee Hays, but everyone calls him Jack. He's the best Indian fighter we've ever had. He leads a ranger company out of San Antonio, but will go wherever he chooses if he catches the scent. Even his own men are in awe of him. They say he'd go to hell and back by himself. If we had two hundred more like him there'd be no Comanche threat in Texas. They'd all be mustered out.'

I was intrigued. For a man like Bannock to be so impressed said much about this Captain Hays. 'I would like to meet him,' I said.

My companion gave a rueful smile. 'I kind of wish we had him with us on this trip.'

His remark was made lightly, but nonetheless I was chilled by it. It seemed to indicate that he was of the opinion we might need help against Braxton and his following, but where could we possibly find any out here?

★   ★   ★

As the sun went down I felt a blessed relief from the day's heat. The temperature was now actually pleasant. We halted for yet another cold camp. Necessary or not, they were getting truly tiresome. 'I would kill for some freshly cooked food,' I complained bitterly.

'If the smell drifted downwind you'd probably have to,' my companion replied laconically. What he said next was much more of a surprise. 'We'll have to stand watch turn and turn about from now on. I'll take the first spell.'

'What on earth for? It's night-time and no one is hunting us.'

He flashed me a pitying look. 'We're the predator, not the prey. Is that it?' Before I could answer he continued, 'You might have noticed that the moon's getting fuller. Up here on the plateau there's nothing to break up the landscape. It's mighty easy for Comanche war bands to travel at night, and I ain't having one of them trip over me unawares.'

Belatedly I understood. 'In that case I will take double duty. You can't have slept much last night so it's the least I can do.'

Bannock flashed me a smile. 'How very noble of you.'

'Bugger off and get some sleep,' I returned, resigning myself to a long night with little rest. I settled down with a piece of beef jerky and some corndodgers as he stretched out on a saddle blanket. One last thought occurred to me. 'Why did Jonas call you Beaujolais?'

Bannock sat up sharply and regarded me through the gloom. 'You saw what happened to that little maggot, didn't you. Learn from it!'

That had touched a nerve, but I was not for backing down. 'Don't be ridiculous. It's a perfectly reasonable question,' I persisted.

Bannock sighed. 'You can be a real pain in the ass! OK, All right. It's my given name, but I never use it. You satisfied now?'

'Beaujolais Bannock! Your mother certainly had a sense of humour,' I cackled.

'You leave my ma out of this and let me sleep,' he growled, settling back on his blanket.

* * *

I slowly came out of a deep but necessarily short sleep and looked around, bewildered. There was a balmy warmth to the day that was very pleasant, and I didn't want to move. I had been as good as my word to Bannock, who had only relieved me a short while before dawn. The night had passed quietly enough.

My brief reverie was soon spoilt by Bannock gargling and spitting in close proximity. I rolled over and looked up.

'Morning, Major. Sun's up, time to move. We need to make up some time today.'

Groaning, I clambered to my feet. Now was not the time to wallow in self-pity. Somewhere out there Sarah was in the hands of ruthless brigands and desperate for rescue. I couldn't contemplate what the future might hold for her if I was to let her down.

The new day proved to be as insufferable as the previous one, with the shimmering heat haze and monotonous pace.

'Do you think we've gained any ground today?' I asked hopefully, as the sun at last descended.

'Possibly,' he allowed. 'It depends on how many trade goods they're toting along as well as the woman.'

'*Trade goods*,' I cried out incredulously.

'Of course. Braxton's a businessman. If he were visiting the Comanches anyway he'd be sure to profit in any way he could.' Looking at me speculatively he continued, 'Now if you could seize him, the 'breed and his contraband together, *and* hold on to them.' He whistled, 'Well, then you'd have Lamar dangling on a hook, wouldn't you?'

I was impressed. He'd obviously given some thought to what I had said two days earlier. Achieving that objective though, would require a lot of luck, and involve a great deal of risk. A man like Braxton would only ever be easy to handle when he was dead. But the idea stayed in my mind as we plodded along to our next campsite.

11

That night began very much like the previous one, but it ended in a way that I could never have foreseen. We settled down on the sun-blasted prairie, and endured the usual mix of cold food, tepid water and desultory conversation. I had drawn the first watch, during which my comrade, for that was how I now viewed him, slept soundly. The night was warm. There was a gentle breeze and the moon bathed the land in its eerie light. Eventually, having served my time, I gently prodded Bannock awake.

Softly he asked, 'All quiet?' The very question showed that he was still woolly with sleep. If it hadn't been, the atmosphere would have been considerably less relaxed. I grunted acknowledgement, then gratefully curled up on my own blanket. I must have been very fatigued, as I dropped off instantly, almost as a candle would be snuffed out.

★ ★ ★

Barely had I slept before I was being shaken awake, but this time there was a difference. A calloused hand was clamped firmly over my mouth. I began to struggle, but was then aware of a voice hissing urgently in my ear. 'Wake up, dammit, and don't make a sound!'

My eyes found his as he gestured off into the distance. Tingling with anticipation, and now free of his grasp, I stared off into the silvery gloom. But at what was I supposed to be looking? Puzzled, I glanced over at him. His right forefinger pointed over my saddle and I looked again, straining to identify the source of his concern.

Then I saw them! Because they had now begun to move again. My skin crawled as the realization dawned on me. A large group of horsemen was steadily approaching our camp, and would surely ride over us unless checked. They were still some distance away and obviously unaware of our presence, but we would have to decide our next move very swiftly. I looked back to Bannock for guidance. Again he whispered in my ear.

'Comanche raiding party. A big one. We can't load up in time to outrun them, so we'll have to make a stand. Give them hard knocks and hope they back off.'

I was aghast at the prospect, but had been with him long enough to know that he was usually correct in his assessments. I nodded. 'All right, I'm with you,' I said boldly, realizing immediately how stupid that sounded, as I had nowhere else to go.

'Give me the scattergun,' he demanded, all the time watching the Indians' unhurried advance. Immediately I complied. If this developed into a battle it would be at short-range, and we would have to hit them with everything. I pulled out both revolvers

177

and laid them in front of me.

As I did so he hissed at me, 'We're seen, cock your pieces!'

The Comanches had come to an abrupt halt, and were now milling around their leader as he tried to make out our numbers and apparent readiness. Silence was no longer relevant, and Bannock laughed out loud.

'I'll bet whoever made us out shit themselves. Look at them. They don't know what to do for the best.'

My guts were in knots and I didn't see any humour in the situation. A thought occurred to me and I called over, 'What about our horses?'

'We can't control them and fight,' he replied. 'If they look like being run off shoot them.'

For a brief glorious moment I thought the Comanches might actually ride around us, but then the ranger bellowed out, 'They're on the move. Defend yourself!'

Their rate of change from total disorder to flat out gallop was awesome, and truly chilling. In the light of the moon they resembled ghostly spectres as they came howling towards our position. It was truly a test of nerve to stand fast in the face of such a charge.

'They're coming full chisel! They'll swing round behind to catch us unawares,' yelled Bannock as he sighted down the barrel of his long rifle. There was a sharp crack, and a Comanche was flung sideways under the thundering hoofs of his companions' horses, testimony to the accuracy of the ranger's shooting. They were now within long pistol range and I lay flat, holding a revolver in a two-handed grip, the barrel resting on my saddle. Taking careful aim at a fast approaching horse I squeezed the trigger, jumping involuntarily as flecks of copper flew back at my eyes, a common occurrence with percussion caps.

Without waiting to see the fall of shot I switched to another target, cocked and fired again. As I did so Bannock discharged the shotgun, the blast temporarily blotting out all other sounds. The field of battle was obscured by powder smoke, but as its deadly load struck I could make out the awful screams of man and beast.

The leaders were now within a few yards, so rising up on to my knees I fired twice more into the approaching mass. Then Bannock released the other barrel of the twelve' gauge into their midst. He was so close to me that I could feel the shock wave. A horse loomed out of the powder haze, its rider searching for a victim for his lance. Pointing the Colt directly up at his face I fired. He was thrown backwards and disappeared into the mêlée.

Empty!

Dropping the revolver like a hot coal I reached down for the other. As I did so Bannock yelled out, 'They're behind us!'

Still on my knees I twisted round. An arrow skimmed past my face whilst another slammed into the saddle. This was truly desperate. The ranger was firing off his single-shot pistols with an icy calm and deadly accuracy. Riderless horses were careering past, adding to the confusion. As if from nowhere a howling banshee leapt at Bannock and plunged a knife into his left shoulder. The savage's momentum sent them tumbling down together. As I turned, the frenzied creature withdrew the blade and thrust it straight at my friend's throat. Instinctively I pressed the muzzle of my revolver to his right ear and squeezed the trigger. The Comanche's head was blown to the side, and he collapsed in a welter of blood and brain tissue. The sickly sweet smell of burning flesh wafted over me.

Abruptly my head seemed to explode in agony, and I slumped forward on to Bannock's legs. What'd hit me? Tasting blood in my mouth, I felt rather than heard the discharge of a gun, mere inches above me. A disembodied voice screamed out, '*Get up, Get up,*' and I was shoved backwards. Rolling on to all fours I tried to rise, but my head was pounding and there was no strength in my legs. Where was Bannock? I couldn't even see anything. Surely this must be the end! My luck had finally run out!

And yet no arrows skewered me, no knives or lances sliced into me. The crescendo of gunfire was reaching a climax, but who could be firing? Gradually my vision cleared, and I looked out on to the moonlit prairie. The surviving Comanches were in full flight, hotly pursued by our saviours, whoever they might be.

Desperately looking around for my companion, I glimpsed a figure stealthily rising up off the ground some few yards away. Clad only in a loincloth! The realization hit me that he had to be an unhorsed savage, left behind for dead by his comrades. Our eyes met and he froze. With chilling clarity I understood that both of us knew exactly what the other was thinking.

Have I got a weapon to hand?

Can I kill him before he reaches me?

As though connected by an umbilical cord we remained locked together by sight, neither daring to be the first to break the spell. Both of us realized that if either looked away in search of a weapon, the other would make a move. I don't know how long we would have remained like that, but events beyond our limited range of vision took over. With joyous whoops the mysterious rescuers returned from the chase, and we simultaneously recognized that time was running out. With an explosion of effort the Comanche leapt to his feet and lunged towards me.

Frantically I searched the ground for anything I could use in my defence. The only thing within reach was the discarded and empty shotgun. I pounced on it, threw it to my shoulder and thumbed back a hammer just as the savage reached me. Clutching a vicious hunting knife, he stopped in his tracks, shock registering on his bronzed face as he stared into the awesome muzzles of the 'two-shoot' gun. I allowed myself a triumphant smile, before slamming the heavy stock into the side of his head. Legs buckling beneath him, the warrior collapsed on to the hard earth and lay there, stunned and bleeding. Sucking in a deep breath to steady myself, I looked up as a group of riders reined in before me.

A bearded figure regarded me with interest as he remarked, 'That's just typical of a Comanche. Brings a knife to a gunfight!' So saying he took swift aim with his revolver and fired two rounds into the prone savage. As I glanced down my jaw dropped at his accuracy. Both eyes had been perfectly drilled, and in the moonlight to boot. My assailant was simultaneously blind and dead.

'By their beliefs he's forever doomed to wander the afterlife like that,' the marksman explained, to the sound of guffaws from a number of his companions.

I felt physically and emotionally

drained. Limply I asked, 'Who on earth are you?'

To my immense surprise Bannock's voice answered from off to the left. 'If you ever had cause to pray to God for deliverance he's who you'd get.'

I regarded my friend with some disquiet, as he was soaked in blood and obviously weak. But he still managed a smile as he gestured towards the bearded horseman.

'Major Thomas Collins, meet Captain Jack Hays!'

12

This man Hays was like no other whom I had encountered in the fledgling republic. He was obviously adored by his followers, and held in high esteem by my own ranger companion. But at first glance he wasn't much to look at. Of similar age to myself he was short, slight and slim-hipped, with a rather high voice, and did not at all resemble a much-revered hero. However, as I observed him interact with his hard-bitten crew, I realized that he had a certain something about him. There was a quiet, calm charisma, an aura if you will, that seemed to surround him like a halo. Following his dramatic shooting display he had vaulted off his horse and moved swiftly over to Bannock's side, concern etched on his features.

'I don't know what brings you to this

god-forsaken spot, my friend,' he said, 'but that bleeding must be plugged immediately.'

He pulled a section of rawhide from a pocket and bound it tightly just above the knife wound in Bannock's shoulder. Then, accepting no refusal, he required Bannock to lie down on his rearranged saddle blanket and proceeded to bath the deep gash from his own canteen, all the while conversing with him in hushed tones. At last he was done, and, speaking quietly and precisely, he announced, 'You appear to be entirely fortunate in that the wound is clean and untainted, but you have lost a lot of blood and must rest.'

To my surprise Bannock just nodded and complied without protest. Turning his attention to me, Hays tilted his head slightly, a smile creasing his weathered face. 'So, *Major* Collins, it would appear that you outrank me, but perhaps you would explain your involvement in all this mayhem.' It was politely put, but there was no disguising the voice of command.

Placing the shotgun on the ground next to me I drew myself up to my full height and formally introduced myself. 'I am Major Thomas Collins, Fourth Regiment of Foot, British Army. I am on secondment to Her Majesty's Foreign Office, and en route to present myself before your President Houston in Washington.' With that said I fell silent awaiting his response.

There were snorts of disbelief from various members of Hays's company, but he silenced these with a glance. Returning his gaze to me, he scrutinized me for a full minute without comment. Everybody else had gone quiet as they awaited his pronouncement. When it came it entirely surprised me.

'I'm satisfied that you speak the truth, but I must press you on one point. If you are travelling to Washington as an accredited diplomat, then why are you knee-deep in dead Comanche warriors so many miles from your destination?'

A twinkle in the eye had accompanied this enquiry, and I realized that I was dealing with a highly intelligent and educated man. And so, as briefly as possible, I told him of Sarah Fetterman and Silas Braxton and of my theory concerning Lamar's involvement. This threw the assembled rangers into uproar, but their leader just continued to regard me in silence.

After what seemed like an age he appeared to come to a decision, and commenced shouting out commands. Soon his men, who numbered approximately twenty riders, were busy about their various tasks. These included slaughtering all the Comanche horses that could be caught, recovering our mounts, destroying the savages' weapons and in some cases scalping our assailants.

Having set all this in motion, Captain Hays solemnly proffered his right hand and said, 'Welcome to the Republic of Texas, Major. I would have words with you regarding your theory, if you would oblige me.' Accepting his grip I nodded my agreement, and we both sat down next to Bannock so that he might be included in the conversation.

'I fully accept your account of Braxton's activities,' Hays began. 'It is totally in keeping with the man's character. My concern is over the matter of General Lamar's connection in all this. He's a former president of the republic, a war hero and responsible for my appointment as captain of rangers. If what you believe is true it would mean his public ruin, and I'm not at all sure that that would be of benefit to this country. After all, whilst I don't condone the attacks upon your person, I have no wish to see the British Empire marching into my country.'

My heart sank and I regarded him intently as I asked, 'So what do you intend to do, Captain?'

'I intend to do my duty!'

'Which is?'

'I am charged with apprehending and destroying hostile Injuns wherever and whenever I may find them. As I've just been informed there's to be a meeting between a band of Comancheros and a group of Pehnahterkuh Comanches, I intend pursuing them with all vigour. What happens after that depends entirely on the outcome.'

I couldn't believe what I was hearing. 'So you do intend to help me rescue Sarah,' I blurted out, following on hastily with, 'And apprehend Braxton and his cronies.'

The ranger captain regarded me shrewdly before answering. 'If you harbour romantic feelings for this lady, I suggest you consign them to the recesses of your mind for the present. Distractions of a sexual nature will get you killed out here.'

Colouring slightly at his directness I moved swiftly on. 'And what of Bannock? He doesn't look strong enough to continue so soon.'

'He can rest up here awhile. Two of my men were slightly wounded in that fracas, so they'll remain with him and follow on in a day or so.'

And so it was settled. I was to ride with Hays and the main body of men. He, like Bannock, felt that Braxton would be making for the San Saba River, which would mean our crossing the Colorado later that day, as we pushed westward. I collected my belongings together whilst he informed his men of their new mission.

After saddling my horse I moved over to where Bannock lay, and knelt down next to him. He reached out and gripped my arm with remarkable strength. 'You saved my hide tonight. We make a good team. So don't go doing anything dumb out there, Thomas!'

Our eyes locked together for a few seconds and I felt a surge of warmth for the man. But the mood was swiftly broken by his next remark. 'Now piss off and kill some white trash for me!'

Laughing, I got to my feet and mounted up. The rangers were moving off; outriders were already well out, ahead of the main body. With a salute I spurred off to join them.

★ ★ ★

For the remainder of that long and eventful night we rode steadily west. There was no talking and some of the rangers appeared to be dozing in their saddles, but nobody drifted or fell behind. At last the sun began to come up behind us, and the night and its attendant horrors retreated. Hays signalled a brief halt so that he could confer with, and rotate the outriders. I took the opportunity to put a question to the ranger captain.

'How were you able to accept so readily my account of who I was, when your men seemed most distinctly sceptical?'

'Oh that was simple,' he said with a dismissive wave of the hand. 'You have what is quite obviously a British accent, and nobody could make up a story like yours. You had to be telling the truth.

'And besides,' he added with a wink, 'I asked your good friend Ranger Bannock!'

We were soon on the move again. It was becoming apparent that the Ranger captain drove his men hard, but also that they readily accepted it. Unlike the British Army, where the rank and file were poorly paid and often reluctant volunteers, these men were fighting against vicious predators for their country's very survival. That would always make a difference. They were a richly varied group. I had come across irregular troops before, but nothing like this company. Their clothing conformed to no uniform that I had ever seen. They wore long coats, short coats, waistcoats and a variety of headgear, even including a top hat. They were without exception unwashed and foul-smelling, which spoke of many long days on the trail, and did not seem to have any obvious hierarchy beyond accepting the captain as their leader. However, their mounts were well cared for and they were all armed to the teeth. This was only to be expected as their very survival depended on it.

Catching the captain's eye I raised a matter that had been troubling me deeply. 'What are your intentions when we come upon his party?'

'That depends on what outcome you hope for. The presence of the lady complicates everything. We can't ride in with guns blazing, yet if we surround them it turns into a siege, with Mrs Fetterman as their bargaining tool. As a military man I'm sure you can see the difficulties.'

I nodded pensively and we both fell silent.

★   ★   ★

Shortly after that exchange a wave from one of the outriders sent the captain galloping off ahead of the column. I noticed that all signals and summonses were carried out in silence. The self-discipline shown by these men was exemplary, presumably born out of years spent living with constant danger.

After conferring briefly Hays returned to the main body.

'The Colorado is up ahead. We'll cross in the usual fashion. Major, I would be obliged if you would remain with me.'

Shortly afterwards we crested a slight rise, and below us stretched the river that I had last crossed approaching the city of Austin. It had only been a few days past, yet it seemed like a lifetime ago. As we splashed across, I longed to jump in and wallow in the sparkling water. Once we had all regained dry land the horses were watered, and we filled our canteens in relays so that there were always a number of rangers with guns at the ready.

I was upriver drinking my fill, thinking sadly how Bannock and the other wounded men would have relished the fresh water, when I noticed one of the outriders returning swiftly. He wore a look of satisfaction on his lean, bronzed face. Reining in he released his mount by the water and reported to his leader.

'We cut trail up yonder, Jack. Seven shod horses and some pack-mules. Half a day, maybe less, ahead of us.'

Glancing over at me Hays remarked, 'So, Major, we're overhauling your prey. Question is, do they know yet that we're tracking them?'

'Is he likely to try an ambush?'

The ranger shook his head. 'This ain't the country for that. No, I think he'll get to the San Saba River and sit on the other side, waiting to see who turns up.'

Abruptly he called out, 'To horse. If we're going to catch these sons of bitches we need to ride.'

13

The San Saba River was two days' ride from our crossing place on the Colorado, and the journey passed without incident. We maintained a steady pace, and for the most part rode in silence. The Rangers were all experienced frontiersmen who knew exactly what was required of them, as much for their own safety as for obedience to their captain. At night no fires were lit, all food was eaten cold and nobody complained. All knew the price they paid for a mistake made out there, so far from the settlement line.

* * *

The new day was, as ever, broiling hot and I welcomed our imminent arrival at the river. I realized that we could not be far off, as there was a noticeable increase in tension amongst our company. Their leader joined me to talk. 'As a soldier you will have noticed a certain edginess amongst my men. The cause is obvious, and I would welcome your thoughts on our situation.'

Speaking with greater certainty than I felt I replied, 'I know exactly what needs to be done, but of course I need your agreement.'

Hays arched an eyebrow but said nothing, so I continued, 'If your men arrive at the river crossing Braxton will be confident in standing you off, if he even has cause to think that you would attack him. Because, let's not forget, he can't know that I have joined you or even that I am alive. If I suddenly appear at the riverbank alone, demanding to see Sarah, he'll be greatly surprised and I believe that his curiosity and arrogance will provide me with a chance to cross over and parley. In the meantime, your best shots will have crossed elsewhere and deployed around Braxton's camp. They will have had to advance on foot because, as you say, this terrain does not lend itself to ambush. Of course all this depends on your cooperation, because, although I outrank you, unfortunately I'm in the wrong country.'

The other man laughed and clapped me on the shoulder. 'I really am getting to like you. It would be such a shame if you were to get slaughtered in front of your lady friend. But all things considered I will do as you ask.'

I thought, *How can it be so easy?* Then I realized. 'You don't want to risk your men,' I blurted out. 'If I'm killed you can pull your rangers back and withdraw without loss. Sarah means nothing to you, and as Lamar's protégée you do not run the risk of finding out that I was right.'

For the first time since I had met him real anger crossed the captain's face. He reined in sharply and sat his horse, staring at me. A nerve twitched under his left eye, and I wondered if I had perhaps gone too far. I was aware that the men around him had also halted, and were awaiting events.

At length he spoke with an enforced calm. 'Yes, you're right. I do not wish to risk the lives of these good men. They've already suffered too much defending this land. But if you think that I would leave you high and dry against the likes of Silas Braxton then you do not know John Coffee Hays. And no man here would leave a female captive with that crew.'

There were murmurs of agreement from all around me as he continued: 'If there is indeed proof that his wrongdoing reaches up to Mirabeau Lamar then we will together present your case to Sam Houston himself. You have my word on that, and if Bannock told you anything about me at all then you will accept it.'

I absorbed all that he'd said, but before I could reply a singularly hard-bitten ranger, somewhat older than the average, began to speak.

'With the cap'n's permission, I mean

to tell you something, Mr English *Soldat*. I ain't got the learning to dress this up in fancy speech, but I'll say this. For a stranger here you run your mouth kind of reckless. If Jack Hays gives his word, he'll go to hell and back before he breaks it, and you'd do well and remember that.'

Hays gave a gentle smile. 'I'm obliged to you for your testimonial, Kirby. It is much appreciated.' Turning his attention back to me he continued, 'So, Major, do we go with your plan?'

Somewhat chastened I replied solemnly, 'I can't think of any good reason why not.'

'Excepting Silas could just gun you down like a dog,' added Kirby with a leer.

★   ★   ★

A short while later the company came to a halt. The outriders were all returning, but slowly so as not to raise too much dust. The first back reported in:

'We seen them, Jack. Far side of the San Saba. Even got a fire going. Could smell the coffee!'

I could contain myself no longer. 'Was there a woman with them?'

The ranger shook his head. 'Couldn't get that close, mister. Looked to be seven of them camped above the riverbank. No way of getting near without being seen.'

'So my idea is the only way to avoid a long-range stand-off,' I pronounced triumphantly. And so it was decided.

Hays, brisk and efficient, specified what was needed. 'There'll be just six of my men crossing, all excellent shots. The rest will remain here with me to back your play once the shooting starts. You must allow my men time to cross over up river and move into position. I believe you are in the right of it, in that Braxton will be both curious about your arrival and over-confident in his numbers.'

The captain moved away to give his orders, and I dismounted to inspect the loads in my weapons. All was well, but I checked again anyway. Having ensured that all the percussion caps were securely seated I could do no more, which was when the stomach gripes started.

'If only I could make my move now,' I reflected grimly. The waiting was always the same. Hays's sharpshooters had moved off, but I had no choice but to stay put. The churning grew worse until I had to walk away from the remaining rangers to squat in the grass and relieve my tortured bowels. As I returned to the main group the ranger leader glanced at me sympathetically.

'The waiting is always the worst of it,' he said quietly.

'You'd think by now that I'd be used to it,' I replied regretfully.

Lying down on the grass I tried to relax and willed the time to pass. At last, after what seemed an age, the captain knelt down next to me and put his hand gently on my shoulder. 'Time to go, Thomas,' he announced.

I got quickly to my feet, took his proffered hand and gripped it firmly.

'Try and slant in from the south-west so that the sun is behind you. It's not much, but it may just give you a slight edge,' he advised.

'I'll do that,' I said, mounting up. 'And thank you, for everything.'

I moved off at a steady pace on the first part of a dogleg course to achieve what Hays had suggested. Now that I was moving at last I felt better in myself. The nerves were still there, but my stomach had settled down. As the rangers receded from view an idea came to me. I reached into one of my saddle-bags and pulled out a spare white shirt. Slowing to a walk, I tied it around the twin muzzles of my shotgun. A flag of truce might just help to confuse the issue, and give me a little more time.

I pulled gently on the reins to effect a right-angle turn so as to bring me up to the San Saba River with the sun at my back. I pulled back both hammers on the gun, I rested the stock on my left thigh and held it vertically, with my left hand both holding it and obscuring the cocking mechanism. My revolvers were jammed into my belt close to my right hand. My horse could sense my anticipation and tried to increase speed, but I held him back to a walk. I really didn't want to take anyone by surprise, although that was likely to be the outcome.

* * *

Eventually I noticed that a short distance ahead the interminable grassland was broken. I was nearly there. Pulling my shoulders back, I sucked in my aching gut and took a deep breath. Before me a gentle slope led down to the river's edge. It was some thirty feet to the far bank, and I prayed to Almighty God that the depth would be manageable. The water seemed to taunt me with its desirability. Sweat was pouring from me, and then the damned 'flag' drifted on to my moist face, destroying any chance of a dignified approach. Suddenly, from across the river, there came a shouted challenge. My presence was discovered, and any chance to turn back had gone.

'I come to talk with you under a white flag of truce,' I bellowed out, desperately brushing the shirt aside as I searched the far bank for my prey.

'That ain't a flag. That's just a pretty shirt from off your back,' yelled a voice from across the water. The speaker was atop the grassy bank roughly opposite me.

'It can't be his, there's no yellow streak on it,' came another voice close to him. I couldn't see either of them, and my advantage of surprise seemed to be slipping away.

Then, after all my efforts to locate him, the man himself appeared.

Rising up from the brow of the grassy bank slightly off to my right, Silas Braxton stood there, large as life, and apparently unarmed. I took in the craggy face with its scar on the left cheek. He looked as hard and unpleasant as I remembered him to be. And there was something else too: a look of triumph.

'Well, look who's turned up,' he sneered, his keen eyes taking in my weaponry. 'Kind of dropped into my lap, you might say.' He paused and searched the surrounding terrain before continuing: 'I don't know how you got past Frank, but you'd better mind how you go, I've got an old friend of yours with me.' He made a gesture off to his right and there was movement. From behind the crest of the riverbank two people rose into view and my heart leapt. '*Sarah*,' I blurted out. 'Don't be afraid. I've come for you.'

She was dirty and bedraggled, and her wrists were bound before her, but to my eyes she looked simply ravishing.

'Thomas,' she cried out. 'Oh God, you've found me!'

Braxton had observed my reaction to her sudden appearance and he nodded, as if agreeing with something. 'That old bat Bullock was right. You're proper smitten with this Dutch gal. And from the way you're loaded for bear, you reckon on having her back.'

'I haven't come to fight you. I wish to trade for her,' I replied quickly.

'Ha, damn right you won't be fighting!' Glancing over at Sarah he called out, 'Boon, show him.'

The man standing directly behind her pulled out a huge hunting knife, and placed the blade at her throat. Rage surged through my body, but I forced myself to appear outwardly calm. I was praying that the time spent over this was giving the ranger captain's six marksmen a chance to get into position.

'That's known as an Arkansas toothpick, Major. If he has call to use it, her pretty little head will be in the dust and you'll have had a wasted journey.'

'That's not necessary,' I said firmly, sounding a lot bolder than I felt. 'I have come here to buy her from you. I understand that is normal practice with Comancheros.'

That word again!

'You just love to prod, don't you? You've got nothing that we want, *and* nothing that we couldn't take from you anyhow,' stated Braxton, but he didn't sound totally convinced.

Whilst we were talking I urged my horse into the shallows of the river, ostensibly to allow him to drink, but all the time I was looking for Braxton's other confederates. My lack of knowledge as to the depth of the water ruled out any prospect of a mad dash across the river. Yet I couldn't allow myself to lose the initiative. Above me Sarah was standing rigidly still, terrifyingly aware of the knife nicking her skin. The sight of her there, bruised and scared, incensed me and I knew it was time to start pushing. I slid my hand down on to the twin triggers of the shotgun and reached for one of the revolvers in my belt.

Braxton's eyes were like flints as he

took this in. 'There's four long irons on you right now, and we've got the girl. Which means we're holding all the aces. You reckon on talking us to death, soldier boy?'

Ignoring him, I stood up in my stirrups and yelled out, 'Any of you wish to surrender?'

Up on the bank top two more faces appeared. '*Say what?*' This was called back in disbelief by one of them.

'Do any of you want to surrender?'

As I spoke I glanced over at Braxton. He was staring at me oddly, as though belatedly realizing that something just wasn't right.

The other of the two faces laughed. 'For a goddamn redcoat you got style. Oh yeah, you got style!'

With almost divine timing a rifle ball slammed into Boon's bovine face, closely followed by another into his neck. Blood splashed on to Sarah, and he was dead before he hit the ground, the knife slipping from his nerveless fingers. I dropped the muzzles of my

211

shotgun, levelled it at the last man to speak and pulled both triggers. With a stunning roar it discharged its lethal load, enveloping me in a cloud of acrid smoke. Aided by the recoil I let it continue on its arc, hurling it behind me on to the grassy bank. From the far side came high-pitched screaming, and I knew that I'd done some damage.

I drew and cocked a revolver and searched for another target. Braxton had concealed a weapon behind his back. As he drew this from his belt another of the hidden marksmen planted a ball in his left thigh, and he crumpled to the ground. He must have been in great pain, but still managed to shout at his remaining men, 'Get the bitch!'

Sarah jumped for the slope just as one of them made a grab for her. Taking rapid aim I fired, mere seconds before my horse dropped from under me. Pitched into the tepid water I tried to stand up, but the river bottom had dropped away steeply and I began thrashing around, losing my revolver in the process. A voice ahead of me cried out in terror. 'Thomas, help me. I can't swim!'

In dodging the man whom I had fired at, Sarah had rolled down the grassy bank and plunged into the river with her hands still tied. Desperately I struck out towards her. I could hear shouting and firing all around me, but I ignored it completely. All my efforts were focused on reaching Sarah. Where in God's name was she? Abruptly her head broke the surface as she kicked out wildly and I lunged for her. Wildly grabbing a clump of hair, I stopped her from going under again. She struggled violently and lashed out at me, but I just managed to maintain my grip. We were close to the far bank, so I towed her bodily towards it. At last I felt firm ground beneath my feet and dragged her, gasping for breath, out of the torrent.

'You damn near tore my scalp off, you madman,' she howled, before flinging herself into my arms. Though her wrists were still bound she nearly knocked me back into the river, but I clung on, hugging and kissing her unashamedly. From the far bank came clapping, and much ribald laughter. The audience proved to be Hays and his rangers. They had come on swiftly at the first sound of gunfire.

'You must introduce me to the lady,' called out the captain. 'But first I need to see who we've got here.' He urged his horse into the water, going waist deep before climbing out on my side. His men followed him, one of them scooping up my shotgun without even dismounting, and they all spurred up the slope to join the six marksmen.

I unsheathed my knife and carefully sliced through Sarah's bonds. She groaned in pain and rubbed her wrists. 'I can't believe it's you,' she said breathlessly. 'I never thought you'd find me before the Comanches took me.'

Before I could reply there came a rapid exchange of oaths from above us, followed by a series of shots. Cocking my revolver I shouted, 'Stay there,' and ran up the slope. In the heat of the moment I was oblivious to the fact that my powder was soaked and therefore useless.

Upon reaching the crest I found a group of rangers gathered round a blood-spattered body. Kirby took in my bedraggled appearance and grinned. 'Looks like you done taken a bath, Major.'

At that all the coiled tension left me, and I flopped down on the grass with a weary smile.

'I'm not the only one.' Turning, I called out, 'All is safe, you may come up now.'

While I waited for Sarah to join me, I looked around at the extraordinary sight that greeted me. There was indeed a campfire burning, so at last I would get some hot coffee. Of the six men that it had served four were dead, Braxton was wounded and there remained one man standing. He was a fearsome-looking half-caste who, under the watchful eyes of two rangers, glared balefully around him at the unwelcome guests.

Hays strode up to me with a look of satisfaction on his face. 'A real fine haul, Major. Bannock was on the nail about you.'

Before I could reply Sarah staggered into view, and the ranger immediately leapt forward to introduce himself. 'You must be Mrs Fetterman. I am Jack Hays and I'm gratified to see you safe and well.'

Giving him a huge smile she replied, 'I can't believe this turn in fortune. What has become of those cursed devils who took me?'

'Four are mustered out, ma'am. The leader, Braxton, took a ball in the thigh and the 'breed is fit as a fiddle. But enough of this talk. You are near drowned and need attention. Kirby?'

'Cap'n?'

'Detail some men to shield off the

fire with blankets while the lady gets out of her wet clothes. They'll face outwards, mind.'

'Your 'druthers' is my 'ruthers', Cap'n,' he replied, a look of disappointment on his face.

Leaving Sarah in many pairs of safe hands I got to my feet and walked, dripping, over to where Silas Braxton lay. No one seemed in the least bit concerned that I was still wearing wet clothes. My enemy was bleeding and obviously in great discomfort, but he was still able to voice his defiance.

'You tarnal asswipe! You'll regret this day.' The scar on his face was livid and his lips were flecked with spittle as he vented his anger. 'Do you know who I am? You won't always have this posse of rangers around to hold your faggot hand.'

With a remarkable lack of concern one of the aforementioned rammed the muzzle of his rifle into Braxton's thigh. No amount of anger could mask the pain. I unsheathed my knife and knelt at his side. Keen anticipation showed on the rangers' faces, and I also detected something resembling fear in the wounded man's eyes. Calmly I spoke to him.

'For reasons that you and I both know you want me dead, whereas of course I need you very much alive. So . . . '

Taking hold of the coarse material I forced the point of the blade into his pants leg and cut up into the cloth.

Protesting angrily, he reached out to stop me, 'What the hell are you doing to my britches with that toad-stabber, English?'

In response I rapped his knuckles sharply with the flat of the blade. 'Unless you want to lose this leg I need to see where the ball is lodged.'

The logic of that cut through his pain and anger, and reluctantly he submitted to my examination. I quickly found both the entry and the exit wounds in the fleshy part of his inner thigh. There was plenty of blood, but it was not life-threatening if treated properly.

'You're very fortunate,' I said. 'It went clean through.'

Relief showed on his hard features. Any man, however tough, would pale at the thought of being probed for a piece of lead. But it was not over for him yet.

'When it hit, the ball took a fragment of cloth into the wound. If it remains in, the leg could become infected.'

Braxton pondered on that and then sneered. 'You're going to really enjoy this, aren't you?'

Without bothering to answer I got up and walked over to the fire. Sarah was wrapped in a blanket while her clothes dried in the sun. It was noticeably lacking in length and consequently she was showing a great deal more leg than was usual. Her admirers were numerous, but she was too delighted by her freedom to bother. As I approached her she beamed at me, and I felt like the happiest man in the world.

'We've got lots to talk about,' I stated

eagerly. 'But first there's something I need to do.'

I placed my knife in the embers of the fire and explained my intentions, reflecting that, even now, I could not get that cup of hot coffee.

My blade was by now glowing. I withdrew it from the fire and returned to my reluctant patient. He lay between his two guards, his hard eyes watching my approach. Seeing the keen cutting edge in my hand, fresh sweat broke out on his forehead, and he favoured me with a sick smile. I realized then that Braxton alone knew what my real intention was.

'I really did underestimate you, English, but I won't make that mistake again,' he remarked bitterly.

Kneeling down, I fixed my gaze on him and spoke quietly. 'I must remove that cloth from your wound if it is to heal. How long this takes is up to you, as I believe you realize.'

'I comprehend what you are about, Bloody Back, but know this. Whatever suffering you visit on me I'll pay back tenfold.'

By way of reply I placed my knife above the wound and used my left hand to part the torn flesh. Steeling myself against his reaction, I eased the burning point into his leg. As the frightful probe penetrated his body Braxton's eyes bulged. He went rigid and emitted a blood-curdling scream. Sweat was pouring from him, and I was conscious of his steely eyes boring into me. Rapidly I withdrew the knife and lowered myself until I was level with his left ear. His whole body was shuddering with reaction, but he listened when I whispered. 'I saw the piece of cloth. It is within reach of my point, but first I need answers to my questions.'

Through his agony he snarled at me. 'You're all shit and no sugar, and you can go to hell!'

'I've already been there,' I hissed, swiftly inserting the blade back into his tortured flesh. Drawing on some inner strength he didn't scream again, but his whole body convulsed, and the sweat continued to roll off his face in torrents.

It proved too much for Sarah. 'Stop, stop it! This is just sick,' she protested, twisting from me to Hays and back again.

My reply surprised them both. 'I agree with you, but this man has twice tried to kill me. He has kidnapped the woman that I love, injured a colleague and conspired with enemies of the Republic. The only way that you, Captain, will assist me further is if he admits to all this. Therefore . . . '

Without further ado I eased the knife back into the open wound. The veins swelled on Braxton's neck and he screamed out, 'All right, I'll talk for Christ's sake. Lamar isn't worth all this grief.'

I withdrew the instrument of torment and waited.

'Yes, I tried to kill you, dammit. And I was paid handsomely to do it. The general don't want either the bloody British or the goddamn US of A in

Texas. Why spill all that blood with Santa Anna to drive out the Mex army, just to hand the country over to someone else?'

Knowing that this was the only time he was ever likely to cooperate I pressed on: 'And why do you need the half-caste, Huerta? What use is he to you?'

He hesitated and I placed the tip of the blade at the edge of the much-abused wound. Seeing my intent he cried out, 'Safe passage! He gets me safe passage to trade with the Comanche.'

Angry muttering broke out amongst the assembled rangers, whose morbid curiosity had drawn them to watch the vicious interrogation. Triumphantly I looked up at Captain Hays.

'There! Now do you believe me? He's a Comanchero, the worst enemy that these men have got!'

The captain was regarding me with vague distaste. 'I can't say that I altogether approve of your methods, Major, but yes, I do believe you.'

'And will you help me?'

'You have given me much to think on. I'll give you an answer in my good time, so don't press me.' He said this with an air of finality that I did not challenge.

I rose shakily to my feet and looked at Sarah. 'Would you oblige me by binding his wound?'

Nodding numbly, she asked, 'The cloth, did you recover it?'

Turning away towards the fire I replied, 'The wound was clear. A small subterfuge, but necessary under the circumstances.'

Braxton howled out with unbridled rage. 'You bastard sodomite. You cockchafing tarnal, you'll die for this!'

The abuse ended abruptly with another howl of agony. Looking back I saw a ranger pouring what resembled whiskey over his leg. Kirby winked at me. 'A waste of good tar water, but we don't want poison in that limb.'

14

The day was well advanced as I sat by the glowing fire, enjoying my third cup of what passed for coffee. The ingredients were dubious, but to me it tasted like nectar. My clothes had nearly dried, the burning heat was subsiding and I actually enjoyed a feeling of well-being. The captain, having made it plain that we were remaining there for the night, had issued various orders and then walked off down the riverbank, lost in thought.

Sarah, as requested, had bound Braxton's wound and then sat down in front of me. There was a little bruising and some minor abrasions on her face, but otherwise she seemed to have emerged remarkably unscathed from her period of captivity. She settled her piercing green eyes on me and started talking.

'What you did to that devil was awful. Nothing stops you, does it?'

I made to answer but she carried on. 'His men wanted their way with me, but he checked them. I know why.'

'So do I. It would have affected the price that he received for you.'

'Maybe, but I think he wanted me for himself.' As she said it she shuddered.

'Either way,' I responded, 'he deserves anything that happens to him, but for now I need him alive.'

Looking at me intently she lowered her voice. 'Back there you told everyone that I was the woman you love. Did you really mean that?'

I put my mug down, reached out and grasped her hands. 'I have risked everything coming into this god-forsaken wilderness looking for you. I ask you, would I have done that for Ma Bullock?'

She gave a throaty laugh. 'You may have eyes for her at that, my brave soldier.'

I favoured her with my best wounded

look. 'You may not know this, but there are some things worse than dying, and that would be one of them.'

She laughed again and then gently removed her hands from mine, indicating by her glance that someone was approaching. Turning, I looked up as Captain Hays advanced on us. His slight frame was moving swiftly, as though he had made up his mind about something. He dropped on to his haunches and came quickly to the point. 'You were right about Silas Braxton's trading with the hostiles. If he is to be believed you may even be right about General Lamar. That presents me with a dilemma. My place is on the frontier. Washington-on-the-Brazos is many days east of here. You are undoubtedly a very brave and resourceful officer, but even you have to sleep sometime. If you were to attempt the journey alone, between them Braxton and Huerta would finish you.'

I made to protest but the ranger held up his hand. 'Let me continue, please.

Therefore I have resolved to accompany you to your meeting with President Houston. Let him determine the outcome. It'll be a difficult decision, but that comes with the job.'

Relief flooded over me. The captain stood up, a slow smile breaking over his features.

'Well, I'll leave you alone for now. I'm sure that you two have much to talk about. We'll break camp tomorrow after sunup. I intend to head back the way we came to hook up with Bannock and the others.' He tipped his hat to Sarah and strode off.

We sat there, the two of us, unspeaking. I felt that I should make some attempt to wrestle with the potential political discord ahead of me, but all I really wanted to do was wrestle with Sarah. As if sensing my conflicting thoughts she asked,

'What are you thinking about, Thomas?'

I coloured slightly and she chuckled. 'Not Sam Houston then, I'll be bound.'

I reached out to her. 'In truth I just

want to hold you and never let go, but it's rather public here,' I said.

Her green eyes sparkled as she answered me. 'It'll be sundown before long. If I should need to freshen up I wouldn't dare go down to the river alone. I nearly died there last time.'

My heart started to thump until I was sure she must hear. I was in a fever of impatience for night to fall. Yet, with my life not under threat, the sun seemed to take longer to slip below the horizon than on any other day. Lust has a strange effect on men. Time moves more slowly as the anticipation builds. Concentration becomes difficult and yet there is a constant need for activity. I found myself cleaning and reloading my weapons beyond any rational need. Sarah, staying by me all the time, seemed to sense my mood and understand it.

In the interminable time to nightfall we talked of many things, she and I. How she had been seized by Braxton, dragged half-asleep from her bed and bundled on to a waiting horse. How she had cried out for me to save her. Recalling my time idling by the river I ached with guilt and remorse, but she swept that aside. 'You could not possibly have known, my love.'

She told of how Ma Bullock had shamefully turned away as she was abducted. Braxton had just laughed and said in a voice loaded with menace, 'Your soldier boy will have his own problems if he comes looking for you, my pretty.'

In turn I related to her how Bannock had rejoined me under mysterious circumstances and was now somewhere out on the plateau, wounded and attempting to rejoin us. And so we talked on as the remains of the day slipped by.

At last the glowing orb slipped below the horizon, and a form of darkness settled over the land. Strangely, after hours of impatience, I felt tongue-tied and embarrassed. This woman's husband was barely cold in the ground, yet here I was apparently expecting her to lie with me. As if to allay my concern she reached out for my hand. Our eyes met in the gloom and she smiled. 'How about escorting me down to the river, Thomas? I'd feel a lot safer.'

Glancing guiltily around, I could see the rangers settling down for the night. Some were stationed in outlying positions to guard against any night attack, and two had been detailed to watch over Braxton and Huerta. But we had been left to our own devices. Like two secretive children we made our way carefully towards the riverbank. Anxious not to end up in the water again, we linked arms and quietly descended the grassy slope. I knew with certainty that we must have been observed leaving the camp, but I no longer cared. Arriving at the water's edge we found ourselves truly alone for the first time. I reached out and caressed her cheek. It was as though I had lit a fuse that could not be extinguished. We fell into each other's arms as I smothered her in kisses. She responded with an urgency that told of a pent-up longing. We dropped on to our knees, all modesty forgotten as our hands explored each other's bodies. And so, with the gloom surrounding us like a cloak, we at last achieved genuine togetherness.

15

'Major, would you favour me with your company? *Now*, please!'

My eyes snapped open. Disorientated, I peered up the slope. Daybreak was upon us, the sky was brightening and John Coffee Hays was in deadly earnest. Sarah was fast asleep by my side, so, grabbing my weapons, I made to climb the grassy bank alone. With noticeable impatience the captain motioned for me to stop. 'You will be ill advised to leave a lady down there.'

Something serious had obviously occurred and all my senses went on to the alert. I turned, knelt down and gently shook Sarah until she looked up at me. Her skin glowed, her hair tumbled over the grass and she looked radiant.

'Good morning,' I said with a smile. 'The captain requires me urgently. You must fix yourself and follow me up to the camp immediately.'

Her expression darkened. She nodded fearfully, looking at the river and beyond with the eyes of someone for whom everything has just changed. 'I knew it was too good to last,' she muttered softly.

Panting slightly, I joined the ranger. 'What has occurred?'

Gesturing out beyond the pickets, he answered grimly, 'We are discovered. A large band of Pehnahterkuh Comanche. Presumably come to trade with your friend Braxton.'

Without answering, I ran for my saddle-bags and extracted the spyglass.

Peering down the tube, Hays settled on the distant riders and studied them for some minutes. Then he snapped it shut, turned to me and sighed. 'About fifty of the varmints. They didn't expect to find us here, so they're confused. We shall add to that confusion and then withdraw. I suggest you pack your belongings and get Mrs Fetterman mounted. I have dispositions to make.'

His compact figure moved off at speed as he called out commands to his men. The fire was kicked out, the pickets pulled back, the prisoners were mounted still bound and under guard, and the company prepared to cross the river in relays.

Silas Braxton appeared rejuvenated as he witnessed the activity. Leering at me he called out, 'They're going to be right down your throat in a minute, soldier boy. Just see if they aren't.'

I bristled with anger, but before I could react Hays swung round and strode rapidly towards him. He drew and cocked his revolver and jabbed the muzzle into the man's right thigh.

'One more word and you'll have another leg wound, only I won't miss the bone. Do you comprehend me?'

The trader paled under the ranger's hard stare and slowly nodded.

Turning away, Hays called out, 'Kirby, to me if you please. Bring your rifle.'

The grizzled ranger joined him at his

235

own speed. I knew that it was not studied insolence, but common sense. If marksmanship is called for the heart rate must remain steady.

'What's on your mind, Cap'n?'

'They're unsure how to proceed, so let's give them something else to think on. I want you to bring one of them down. The rest of you, as soon as he fires, cross the river.'

Kirby studied the savages as they milled about, arguing amongst themselves. Their dilemma was obvious. They had come to trade with half a dozen Comancheros, but instead had found a score of undoubtedly hostile Tejanos. They were some 300 yards distant, and obviously considered themselves beyond reach of our guns. The ranger spat a stream of tobacco juice into the earth and called over to one of his comrades. 'Yo Travis, help me hurry one of those fools to eternity.'

The other man sidled over to hunch up in front of Kirby. After cocking his long rifle, Kirby placed the barrel on his assistant's right shoulder and took careful aim. As he did so I remembered my own musketry training from many years past. *Always remember, windage and elevation, Mr Collins. Windage and elevation.*

Breathing slowly and steadily, the ranger squinted down the barrel. He wore a look of calm concentration on his face, as though the outcome was never in doubt. Finger tightening on the trigger, he took a deep breath, held it and squeezed. With a loud crack the heavy lead ball was gone. Everybody present seemed to freeze in anticipation before breaking out in a wild cheer as, in the distance, a Comanche warrior tumbled off his horse and lay still.

'That was damned good shooting, Ranger Kirby,' called out Hays as he mounted up.

'Thank you, Cap'n, thank you kindly.'

★ ★ ★

We had soon all crossed the San Saba River safely and good progress was made. The intention was to meet up with Bannock and his companions, cross the Colorado, descend the Balcones Escarpment and then, having skirted the city of Austin, make directly for Washington-on-the-Brazos.

That sounded simple enough in the planning, but, as with all military manoeuvres, the execution could throw up all kinds of difficulties. The fifty or so Comanche warriors who were carefully shadowing our advance were the most immediate problem. Under the circumstances, Captain Hays seemed remarkably sanguine.

'So, Major Collins, how is Mrs Fetterman standing up to all her adventures?'

I glanced back at her fondly before replying: 'In truth, Captain, quite remarkably well, considering everything she has endured. I have suggested to her that she should stop off at Austin, but she flatly refuses. Some of Braxton's bully boys may remain there and she prefers to accompany me, whatever the perils.'

Hays gave me a calculating look, appeared to be on the point of speaking, then obviously thought better of it. On the point of encouraging him, I was forestalled by a shout from the head of the column.

'Three riders coming in, Cap'n. Look like Anglos to me.'

Our conversation forgotten, the ranger urged his horse to the van and unbidden I followed. Slowly the two groups came together, and my heart leapt as I recognized Bannock. He looked hot and tired, but was sitting his horse well. After exchanging insults and catcalls with the rangers he shook hands with Captain Hays, then dismounted to stretch his legs. As I joined him he looked me up and down, then slapped me on the back. There was no disguising his pleasure at seeing me again. Winking broadly at me he said,

'You're looking mighty chirpy, partner. I see you found your lady friend.'

Before I could reply there came a howl of anger from the rear. Turning rapidly I saw Silas Braxton, astride his horse, his face a picture of pure malevolence. His hands, still bound together, were pointing directly at Bannock. '*You!* It can't be. I saw you die!'

With a half-smile the ranger shook his head. 'The devil is really beating his wife today.'

What that meant I had no idea, and I wasn't about to find out. The captain was keen to move on. 'I'm aware that you've been through the mill, my friend, but we're sorely pressed and need to be on our way.'

'Fair enough, Cap'n. But have you considered a charge to drive them off?'

Hays smiled but shook his head. 'That won't answer. I have two prisoners and a female to consider. Our horses are well used, and we have a deal more distance to cover. My intention is to make the escarpment, then use the cover against them.'

So began the long enervating trek back to the Balcones Escarpment. At no time on that journey were we free of danger. The moonlit nights were insufficiently dark to cloak our movements, so we had to remain continually alert against a night attack, when the range advantage of our rifles was neutralized. Fortunately Kirby's little demonstration had made them wary of our capabilities. Because of the proximity of the Comanches, Braxton and the half-caste Huerta had to be kept permanently bound. The level of hatred displayed by both of them to Bannock was quite astounding, completely eclipsing anything shown to me. Strangely, he would not be drawn into disclosing the reason for this, and yet again I had an uncomfortable feeling that he was holding back from me.

16

At last, worn and dusty, our party arrived at the crest of the Balcones Escarpment, and immediately the terrain and its environment changed. Clusters of trees were visible as the ground began to tail away out of sight. My spirits lifted as I realized that we would at last be able to shake off our pursuers. According to the rangers their behaviour had been highly unusual. Normally, Comanche raiding parties would swoop in, looting and killing before retiring rapidly back to their own lands. But on this occasion they had dogged our footsteps for days, sometimes barely visible but ever present. All of which suggested that we possessed something that they wanted badly: namely Silas Braxton and the Comanchero Huerta.

Now at last, late in the afternoon of

another hot, dry day, we were about to drive them off for good. Captain Hays reined up beside me, a twinkle in his eyes. That man's indomitable spirit had instilled everyone with courage throughout the long, enervating journey back from the San Saba River.

'Major, I intend for us to make a stand. Sarah and the two prisoners will continue down the escarpment with Bannock. If those devils really want them they will have to come through us. You would oblige me by forming up with the rearguard. Your undoubted skill with that scattergun is just what we require. What do you say to that?'

'I would be honoured. I am heartily sick of their presence.'

The advance party began threading their way down the escarpment through the trees. The rest of us, some sixteen in all, dismounted in a grove of junipers and spread out in a rough line. One man securing four horses left twelve fighting men to repel the Comanches, hopefully once and for all. Crouching amongst the much anticipated foliage I felt the familiar tension grow in my gut. All around me the rangers were no doubt enduring similar feelings as they checked their weapons. The savages had halted just beyond effective rifle range to debate the change in circumstances.

'Come on, you varmints,' muttered Kirby, kneeling off to my right. Sarah and the others were well away by now, but still the Comanches held their distance. 'What you reckon, Major? Are they going to make a fight of it or what?'

I looked over at him in surprise. A seasoned Indian fighter was asking my opinion. I felt a warm glow of companionship, which can only be experienced by those sharing a common danger. 'I truly hope so,' I answered. 'I'm heartily sick of being shadowed by those devils.'

Kirby nodded approvingly as he spat out a stream of tobacco. It was some minutes before I realized that my stomach was no longer in turmoil.

Abruptly a voice cried out, 'They're on the move!'

I pulled back both hammers and readied myself to receive the charge. This was the part that required both nerve and discipline, as I would have to hold fire when the rangers opened up. The fifty or so Comanches were some 200 yards distant and closing fast. Their horses were kicking up a cloud of dust, which seemed to increase the actual size of the band.

One hundred yards out, just as Hays was about to give the command to open fire, the band of hostiles abruptly fragmented. Moving individually, without any apparent formation, they streamed down on our flanks.

Demonstrating his supreme self-confidence, the captain stood up for all to see and called out calmly: 'Now don't scare, boys, we'll whip them yet. I want you in a circle, horse-holders in the centre. Move!'

Swiftly the rangers formed up as ordered. Hays called out to me. 'Fire in your own time at the largest concentration.'

They were almost upon us. We were now in a close circle around the horses, using the juniper trees for cover wherever possible. The thunder of 200 unshod hoofs reverberated through the ground, as the Comanches swept in. Their horsemanship was astounding as they negotiated scattered trees at speed. They had to be amongst the finest light cavalry in the world.

After a single volley the rifles were set aside, and every man reached for his Paterson Colt revolver. My luck was in, as right before my eyes a number of Comanches bunched up. Aiming at the centre of the group I took a deep breath and squeezed both triggers. Copper particles flew at my face as the caps disintegrated. The recoil was ferocious as the contents of both barrels tore into the heathen devils. Powder smoke obliterated the scene, but the screams testified to my accuracy. Three unburdened but blood-spattered horses continued to circle our group.

With no time to reload, I dropped the heavy gun and grabbed my revolver, just as the rangers opened fire with their own. Lacking these weapons we would surely have been overrun. A tremendous fusillade ensued, as all around me battle was joined, each man attempting to cover his neighbour's flank. The lingering smoke and fluid nature of the conflict made this exceedingly difficult.

The fight rapidly degenerated into individual struggles for survival. Having discharged two chambers, I was abruptly barged to the ground as a Comanche broke through the defensive ring. After skewering a horse holder with a barbed arrow he sat astride his mount, and gave out a howl of triumph. If he was allowed to run off our horses we were all finished.

As I lay there gasping for breath I instinctively snapped off a shot at the largest target. Struck in the hindquarters, the horse whinnied with shock as its back legs gave way. Its rider, displaying lightning reflexes, threw himself clear and came to his feet before me. Having also regained mine, I thumbed back the hammer. Reacting immediately, the savage hurled his bow at me and then, drawing a knife, lunged forward. As I twisted to swat the bow aside my revolver's barrel clashed with his blade which was reaching for my vitals.

His momentum carried him on to me and together we tumbled back to the ground. We each seized the other's right wrist and lay there, locked in a grunting, snarling struggle for survival. His weight was bearing down on me, but with the ground under me as a buttress I was able to hold him off.

So intense were our efforts that the battle around us all but receded. Sweat dripped from his sun-bronzed face on to my own, as the Comanche tried desperately to gain the advantage. His eyes, black as coals, burned into mine as he exerted ever greater pressure.

Abruptly his head went back and I strained my own to the side to avoid a butt to the face.

It never materialized. With a terrible thwack a rifle stock slammed into the side of his head. Instantly his body went limp and flopped lifelessly off me. Gasping from the effort of the struggle I lay there, watching as a ranger smashed the butt of his gun down on to the prostrate man's skull. Grinning down at me he yelled, 'This isn't over yet. Get on your damn feet!'

The sounds of warfare came flooding back, and I heaved myself upright. The remaining horse-holders had retained control of their charges, as the rangers' superior firepower appeared to be turning the tide. The rough circle had held, and there were many riderless horses careering about. Adding to our defiance, I discharged the remaining two chambers in my revolver and then recovered a rifle from the dead horseholder.

The Comanche encirclement was

disintegrating, as individual warriors broke away with cries of dismay.

Recalling Bannock's words at the Fetterman farmhouse I realized that, despite their overwhelming numbers, the fearsome savages had decided that their magic had failed them and all was lost.

Miraculously I had come through another vicious confrontation unscathed, though not so the Texas Rangers. They had two fatalities and three wounded, but nevertheless we had undoubtedly won a decisive victory. All about us lay dead or dying Comanche warriors.

'They won't be back,' yelled out a triumphant Ranger Kirby. 'I'd stake my old man on it!'

'You might as well for all the use it gets,' called out another.

The sadness of our losses couldn't dampen the exhilaration felt by the survivors. Recognizing the signs, Captain Hays allowed his men a few minutes to 'let off steam', as they swiftly finished off the wounded Indians. That was a relatively new expression, reflecting the rise of modern technology. Approaching me as I reloaded my weapons he said, 'When you've finished I'd be obliged if you'd locate the vanguard and apprise them of our situation. They'll be on hot rocks about now.'

'It will be my pleasure, Captain,' I replied. 'I've had some experience of small-scale conflicts, and I must tell you that your men acquitted themselves admirably today.'

'Why, thank you, Major, and I believe I have you to thank for preventing our horses from being driven off.'

Inclining my head in acknowledgement I replied, 'I acted solely on instinct. Any of your men would have done the same, but I thank you for your kindness all the same.'

The captain departed to attend to the sad task of burying his men. At length, gripping my recharged shotgun, I collected my horse and led it down the slope in search of Sarah. For in truth she was the only person of concern to me just then.

At last I glimpsed her, peering anxiously back up towards the plateau. The sounds of battle must have been a torment to her, a thought that selfishly gave me some comfort. It reinforced my conviction that her feelings for me were genuine. Hurrying towards her I cried out, 'It's over. We drove them off.'

Relief flooded over her lovely features as we embraced.

'Now ain't that just a lovely sight,' sneered Silas Braxton, lying on the ground, wrists shackled.

His guard spat wearily and glanced down at him. 'If you don't hush up, I'm gonna open up that wound for all to see.' Then, turning to me, he enquired, 'Is that the word then? Old Jack's given them another licking?'

Thinking it best not to allude to casualties I merely replied, 'Yes, he's following on soon.' After scanning the group I turned back to Sarah, as she continued to beam up at me with unashamed relief, and asked, 'Where's Bannock?'

Her expression suggested that I should already know. 'Said he needed to make Austin 'lickety split'. Him and Cap'n Jack worked it out between them.'

'Sometimes I don't have the slightest idea what you're talking about, my dear.'

Braxton's guard chuckled. 'Ain't that always the way with womenfolk?'

*   *   *

'We need provisions and he reckoned he had business there. He intends to cache our supplies beyond the city limits. That way we can avoid riding through Austin. It might not fool anybody, watching Bannock leave with such a large amount of vittles, but at least they won't know exactly where we are.' This from Captain Hays, as he rode alongside of us. Although it was the day after that last climactic battle

253

with the Comanches, this was the first time that I had managed to catch him alone. We were now clear of the escarpment and back on level ground. Our exertions on the plateau somehow seemed a world away.

Listening to the ranger captain I felt a worm of anxiety in my gut. Bannock's continued efforts on my behalf showed that I could trust him beyond all doubt. And yet, an aura of mystery surrounded the man to such an extent that I felt a need to probe for answers.

'I'm puzzled as to why he just departed without a word. In fact a lot about that man puzzles me.' As soon as I had uttered those words it occurred to me that I was probably confiding in the wrong person. After all, I was the outsider here, merely a fleeting visitor to this country. Which was possibly how Sarah viewed me. *God*, I thought. *Why does life have to be so complicated?*

The captain chose not to comment, so I changed tack. 'How long do you estimate before we reach Washington?'

'Three to four days, heading east. We should come across your elusive friend again soon.'

★ ★ ★

As it turned out my 'elusive friend' again demonstrated his ability to surprise me. Alerted by the ranger who was riding point, we saw a figure in the distance. As we drew closer it soon became apparent that it was not Bannock. This man was far too small in stature.

'Charles,' I shouted out. 'By God, it's Charles Elliot!'

And so it proved to be. Standing with his horse next to a pile of supplies, the little man was wreathed in smiles. Casting formality aside he ran forward to shake my hand.

'Thomas, Mrs Fetterman, it is indeed a pleasure to see you both again.'

I dismounted, grasped him by the shoulders and carefully inspected his face. The bruise on his forehead was receding, and the splinter wound to his right cheek was healing nicely.

I shouted back down the column, 'Do you see here, Braxton? Another Englishman whom you couldn't kill.'

'There's time enough yet,' that man replied with a hollow smile.

Placing her hand on Elliot's arm Sarah spoke softly, 'I'm truly pleasured to see you looking so hunky-dory, Charles. And my name's Sarah!'

The little man beamed back at her. 'Why that's so very kind of you, Mrs Fetterman — *Sarah*.'

Once Elliot had been introduced to Captain Hays, the ranger was quick to come to the point.

'I'm glad to make your acquaintance, Mr Elliot, and I'm powerful relieved to see those provisions, but where is Ranger Bannock?'

'A most curious fellow, if I may say so. He pounced on me at the Bullock Hotel, bundled me out without even paying, and then abandoned me out here. I've no idea what Mrs Bullock thought of it all. He rode off stating that he had business elsewhere, and that he would meet you in Washington. I'm just glad that you found me. I couldn't hope to have moved all this by myself.'

'Well, Mr Elliot, we are indeed all proceeding to Washington, which will involve some days of hard riding.' Looking dubiously at the rather battered little man Hays asked, 'Do you consider yourself up to the task, sir?'

With a slightly wounded air Elliot replied swiftly, 'I understand that you mean no offence, Captain, but I am an Englishman and will not show myself lacking on a horse. I was born to ride, sir!'

17

Washington-on-the-Brazos!

An elaborate, even grandiose name for what was in reality just another ramshackle frontier town. It was located near to a ferry crossing on the Brazos River, close to its junction with the Navasota River. The ferry had been the impetus behind the growth of the settlement, which had, in the 1820s, been known as La Bahia. The Texas victory at San Jacinto had brought a rapid influx of settlers, although permanent residents could still only be numbered in their hundreds. It was currently the nation's capital, and even boasted its own newspaper: the *Texas National Register*. The accommodation looked as rough and ready as that in Austin, but at least I at last had a chance to pursue my mission.

The arrival of such a large and varied

group of horse aroused much interest amongst the population. To Elliot I said quietly, 'Charles, we must contrive to meet the president at the earliest opportunity. You are acquainted with him. Can I leave it up to you to make the arrangements?'

The little man nodded enthusiastically. He was saddlesore and weary, but his spirits had lifted now that we were back in something akin to civilization. This was far more his *métier* than taking part in gunfights with assassins. 'I will see who is available,' he agreed.

As he moved swiftly off on foot I gratefully dismounted and, standing in the dusty, unpaved thoroughfare, stretched and massaged my back. If I could just successfully conclude my mission here then I could let a steamer transport me back to Galveston in relative comfort. But what of Sarah in all of this? As though we had been thinking in tandem I looked up to find her eyes searching mine. Her lovely face registered both fatigue and anxiety.

Giving her a gentle smile I said, 'Whatever happens in this city we *will* be together.'

'That's what I long for,' she replied. 'But I reckon I'll look up my kinfolk while I'm here. It'll do no harm.' Which was her way of informing me that she wasn't taking any chances. She had been hurt enough recently.

Taking hold of her hands I responded in deadly earnest. 'You go ahead and do what you think fit, but know this. I have lost you once already; I'll not let it happen again.' I held on to her until she nodded slowly. 'How will you find your relative?'

'There's a post office here some-where, they'll know something.' She smiled brightly as she turned her horse away, but I could not rid myself of a lingering uneasiness.

★ ★ ★

To avoid periodic flooding, Washington had been developed on cliffs above the western bank of the Brazos River. The buildings were constructed predominantly of timber, although I remarked on a number of brick-built structures that gave the metropolis an air of permanence. To my disappointment there was no accommodation available anywhere, due to the Texas Congress being in session, so I was left with no choice but to set up camp with the Ranger Company. Pitched on lush grass next to the river, it was a perfect spot for a leisurely picnic, but I did not relish the thought of yet more nights on hard ground. My dismay must have been evident to Captain Hays who had been organizing the deployment of his men.

'The lack of a 'lie back an' sigh' bed is really gnawing on you, isn't it, Major?'

On the point of replying I was interrupted by a stunningly loud report from somewhere on the Brazos. Having travelled to Galveston on board the steamship *Sirius* I immediately recognized the sound. It was a steam horn and very close to hand.

'That'll be the *Mustang* steam craft,' said the captain, straining to catch a glimpse. 'I've heard of it but never seen it.'

That was about to change, as no sooner had he spoken than the *Mustang* slowly hove into view, gleaming white and belching smoke. It was a breathtaking vessel to behold, like some sort of man-made beast. The river was wide, but to my awestruck gaze the ship appeared to fill it. The horn blasted again and, as though answering a summons, townsfolk began to line the riverbank. I had seen many ships in my travels, but never anything as distinctive as that.

At the front were two jet-black chimneys, which seemed to give it a menacing look. It rode very low in the water, and boasted three decks with a single paddle wheel at its rear. This differed markedly from the *Sirius,* which was a high-sided ocean-going ship with twin paddle wheels amidships. Then I realized that, just as we were observing it from the shore, there were people lounging on the decks watching us.

To Hays I remarked, 'Of course, there will be bedrooms on board for the paying passengers.' An idea was taking shape. Maybe I would not be sleeping outdoors that night after all.

The steamer continued upriver for a short distance before swinging round 180 degrees. Moving very slowly now, it gradually eased over towards the riverbank where all the gawkers and idlers stood, taking in the sight. The huge stern wheel had almost ceased its revolutions. The steamer captain could be seen in his wheelhouse above the upper deck; his head was bobbing up and down as he rapidly gauged the distance from the bank and shouted orders to his crew. Eventually the boat came to rest, and eager hands grabbed the ropes to tie them off on trees lining the river.

The ranger captain was obviously entranced by the whole procedure. He spent his life on horseback in the trackless wastes, hunting down enemies of the republic. Something as exotic as this was completely beyond his experience.

For some time the craft and its environs were a hive of activity as people and cargo were unloaded, but eventually calm began to prevail and I made my way down to the planking that had been roughly laid to facilitate access. Stepping lightly on board, I immediately became aware of the slight movement underfoot, which was reminiscent of my sea voyage some weeks before. I felt quite sure that I would be sleeping in comfort that night, but as ever events conspired against me.

*   *   *

It was longer than I expected before Elliot reappeared. Fully two hours passed before he stood before me again, but the broad smile on display between his mutton chop whiskers said it all.

Even the scar on his cheek appeared less livid.

'The President will see us now,' he told me; then, calling out to Hays, he said, 'Captain, a word with you, if you please.' Even his voice carried with it more authority. As the ranger joined us Elliot continued, 'You are to accompany us to the President with the prisoners and a suitable guard.'

Captain Hays fixed his pale-blue eyes on mine and questioned quietly, 'Do you really want to go ahead with this, Major? Once your story gets aired you'll have made a very powerful enemy.'

Even in that warm, tranquil environment I could feel a chill descend on me. 'But what about you and your involvement in all this. Won't you also be in jeopardy?'

The captain's reply demonstrated just how deep his seam of self-confidence ran. 'I live my life on the edge of civilization, permanently courting danger. If anybody wants me they will have to come looking.'

So this was it. The moment of no return. Looking over at the hard, grim features of Silas Braxton I knew there was really no choice in the matter. 'I have journeyed long and hard to meet your president, so let us be about our business.'

Nodding sombrely Hays swivelled on the grass and called out. 'Kirby, to me if you please.'

When that ranger joined us the instructions were brisk. 'The prisoners are to entertain the general. I want you and two others to watch over them, and no spitting on the damn floor. Let's be about it.'

Kirby swallowed back some chewing tobacco and gave a slow smile.

18

At long last, after expending so much time and effort, I found myself standing before Samuel Houston, formerly commanding general and now President of the Republic of Texas. His appearance alone seemed to qualify him for that role. I was reminded of Buford's slightly exaggerated description of him. At well over six feet, broad and straight-backed, he towered over everyone else present. His hair was grey and thinning on top, and I would have put him at about fifty years of age. There was a natural dignity about him, and I felt an immediate empathy with the man, who was to many a living legend.

His keen eyes swept over the eight of us as we crowded into the simple meeting-house, situated to the north of the town. His gaze took in the chained prisoners, the ranger guard, twinkled briefly at Captain Hays and eventually settled on me. For possibly a full minute there was absolute silence as he absorbed my appearance. Such was the great man's presence that nobody thought to interrupt his scrutiny by talking. Only when he had seen enough did he speak.

'Major Collins, for the political envoy of such an influential foreign power you are fairly bristling with weapons. Do I take it that your journey here has been a difficult one?'

'Considering the number of attempts on my person, I think that would be something of an understatement, sir. It would also explain the number of people accompanying me today.'

The president gave me a dry smile and then looked directly at the ranger captain, as if suddenly noticing him for the first time. 'It gives me pleasure to see you again, Captain Hays, but I must admit to some surprise at finding you so far from San Antonio. Are there no Comanches to do battle with at this time?'

Silas Braxton could contain himself no longer. Noticeably favouring his injured leg, he thrust forward, shouting out, 'Damn right there are, General, but this cur took it on himself to arrest a law-abiding citizen of Texas, with no good cause. It ain't right I tell you, not right at all!'

President Houston, hands on hips, turned slightly to scrutinize the source of this interruption. From the expression on his face he was singularly unimpressed.

'I have no intelligence as to who you may be, sir, but let me tell you this. If Captain Hays, in whom I place implicit trust, chooses to clap you in irons then I am sure that he has good reason. Therefore, until I am in possession of all the facts, I will thank you to remain silent.'

Braxton scowled but held his peace. Even so obdurate a character could see the folly of antagonizing the president. Turning to me again, the President adopted a more agreeable expression and continued. 'I think it is time that I was apprised of all that has befallen you since arriving in this republic. Captain, I suggest that you install your prisoners in the adjoining room under guard.'

Following their removal from the room, Houston flung off his frock-coat and stretched out his large frame in a reclining chair. He waved at the three of us and boomed, 'Please, please gentlemen, relax. I feel that the major here has a tale to tell, and we may as well be comfortable.'

Conscious as I was of having the great man's full attention, my mouth dried and my stomach began to flutter. Addressing assembled troops was one thing, a president in office something entirely different.

'In your own time, Major.' This gentle prompting from Houston pushed me into marshalling my thoughts, and the words began to flow. As I got into my stride all my nerves left me. I was no longer aware of the presence of

Secretary of War Hockley or Captain Hays. My attention was focused solely on the man sitting before me. How long I talked for I have no idea, but through my entire discourse the President listened in silence, not once interrupting me. As I described Britain's offer of military and financial aid in exchange for a cotton monopoly his expression never altered, and I was convinced that he already knew. As I related the death of Buford LeMay, the injury sustained by Charles Elliot and the kidnapping of Sarah Fetterman his jaw tightened.

The biggest change in his demeanour came when I aired my suspicions regarding Mirabeau Lamar's involvement. He sat forward in his chair, hands clasped tightly, eyes locked on mine.

Finally I was done and I felt an almost unbelievable lightness of spirit. It was as though, having unburdened myself to a higher authority, the pressure of all that responsibility had left me. Except that this higher authority could quite possibly be hostile to my theories, and my troubles could be just beginning.

Abruptly the president stood up and began to pace the room, completely absorbed in thought. I glanced over at the little figure of Charles Elliot. He favoured me with a nervous smile. He obviously wasn't sure whether I had done the right thing in speaking so candidly. Secretary Hockley, a dour, sober individual, ignored me completely. He was obviously awaiting some sign from his superior. No such caution afflicted Captain Hays, who conferred a broad smile upon me.

After some minutes Houston stopped his pacing, perched himself on the edge of a table and began speaking. 'I am grateful to you, Major, for recounting so fully your experiences in my country. You have touched on a number of issues, which I will address separately. Firstly, the offer of your country's involvement in mine. The sums of money that you mentioned are indeed generous, as indeed is the proposal for military assistance, although I cannot but think that this may be limited to the cotton-growing areas only, therefore falling short of what we require. Be that as it may, your submission will require serious debate by the whole cabinet, a process that will necessarily take some time.'

I had fully expected that response, but even so it was a disappointment. I made to speak but the President held up his hand. 'Pray let me continue. I will give you ample opportunity for discussion afterwards. Now, moving on to your own experiences. I deeply regret all that has befallen you since your arrival in Galveston. The general lawlessness of this country is appalling, although it does appear that there has been a concerted effort by certain persons to hinder your progress. What I find most disconcerting are the allegations that you have made regarding General Lamar. If there were any substance to these, it would have to result in charges being brought against him. As he is a former president of this republic that would do our international reputation no good at all. So, Major, as you may be aware that I have had some experience of practising law, present your case!'

It had finally come to it, but suddenly my absolute certainty was wavering. It was quite obvious that Samuel Houston was a patriot, a proud, strong personality, and revered by his people. But he was also a consummate politician who would do what was required to stay in office. I had yet to decide whether bringing Lamar down benefited my mission. That would depend on whether it benefited the President. But first I had one question of my own. 'Before I proceed, Mr President, I must know one thing. Why, if Washington has been the capital for two years, was I led on such a dangerous and circuitous journey here via Austin?'

The President regarded me calmly as he replied. 'I had absolutely no idea that you were in the republic, or I would certainly have taken steps to ensure your safe arrival.'

My mind was now quite made up. 'The prisoner who berated you is called Silas Braxton. He is an assassin in league with the Comancheros, who at the behest of Lamar has made three attempts on my life. He admitted as much to Captain Hays here, when we accosted him at the San Saba River. He also kidnapped a lady with whom I have formed an attachment, with a view to selling her to the Comanches.'

The President gave a wry smile. 'You have led a busy life during the short time that you have been in this country.' Then turning to the ranger he asked, 'Is this true, Jack? Did this Braxton admit his involvement with Lamar?'

'It was under severe duress, Mr President, but yes he did.'

'How severe?'

'More than you could stand, sir.'

Houston looked at me guardedly.

'You appear to have a strong ruthless streak in you, Major, that could well have jeopardized the admissibility of Braxton's confession in court.'

'Sir, he was not going to admit to anything up to that point.'

The President stared at me, then slammed his hand down on the table. 'God damn it to hell!' Turning to Secretary Hockley he barked out, 'Are you aware of the General's whereabouts at this time, George?'

'I believe he's on one of his hunting expeditions.'

Houston grunted. 'I wish to speak with him at the very earliest opportunity.' Turning back to me he continued, 'You have provided me with much to think on, Major Collins. This will necessarily take some time. Do you have rooms in the city?'

'There were none to be had sir. I have however managed to obtain a stateroom on the steamer *Mustang*. I understand that it remains here for two nights. After that I will be sleeping under the stars again.'

The President favoured me with a broad and genuine smile. 'We can't have Her Majesty's envoy sleeping rough. Come the time, I will see what can be done.'

The audience was concluded. I was about to follow the others through the door, then I held back, stopped and turned. 'Mr President, forgive me, but I do have one more question if you please. Have you heard of a ranger by the name of Beaujolais Bannock?'

His head jerked up abruptly from contemplating the floor. 'A most unusual name, even for these times. I think I would know if I had. Good day to you, Major.'

I departed from the meeting-house feeling distinctly uneasy. Whatever else Samuel Houston was, he had proved himself to be an adept dissembler.

19

Sarah Fetterman watched me carefully as she spoke. Her eyes held an emptiness that I hadn't seen before, not even after the attack on her farmhouse. 'My cousin died of the yellow fever two years ago. Fit as a rutting buck one day, then dead three days later. None of his kin knew where I was to be found. The money ran out along with their luck, and they moved back East. So that's it; I'm all alone.'

'No you're not!' I almost shouted the words. Again I was touched by her aura of both resilience and vulnerability. Lowering my voice I continued, 'Have I not sufficiently declared my intentions to you?' She made to speak, but I placed a finger on her lips. 'No, please let me finish. I wished no ill on your cousin, but do you really think his passing makes any difference? I could not just leave you here, whatever the circumstances. I have managed to obtain staterooms aboard the steamer for the two of us and Charles. They will suffice for the present. As the day is advanced I suggest we obtain some food before repairing on board. We can talk more of this later.'

★   ★   ★

It came about that only the three of us went in search of an inn to satisfy our hunger. Captain Hays insisted on dining with his men. I had offered him the use of our temporary accommodation but he had declined. Apparently he wished to remain with his ranger company, and to ensure that the prisoners had been safely locked away in the storeroom that now served as a gaol. I could not resist the thought that perhaps he was distancing himself from my little group.

Nonetheless I was happy to reacquaint myself with chicken fried steak, and ate like a king for the first time in many days. Sitting back, amidst the swirl of noise and activity in the eating-house, I recalled the last time that I had enjoyed that dish in company with Charles Elliot. As then, he was now seated opposite me; appearing weary and a little battle-scarred, but otherwise in good health. Looking at him speculatively I enquired, 'Are you still carrying that pocket piece, Charles?'

His face went ashen as he stared at me across the table. 'Oh my God! You don't mean it could happen again?'

Sarah, looking up quickly from her food, was mystified by his reaction. But as he touched his scar in recollection she suddenly understood. 'Thomas, what are you saying? That we're all in danger?'

Nodding grimly I leaned forward and lowered my voice. 'I would place a large wager that General Lamar already knows of our presence here, and that as a consequence he feels under threat.

Our disappearance would remove that threat whilst also relieving the President of having to make some awkward decisions. So it occurs to me that now more than ever we are in great peril.'

Elliot sat there looking stunned. He pushed his plate away and asked, 'When is all this all going to end?'

'When the President has decided on what course of action to follow, in relation to both Lamar and the British Empire,' I answered. 'Until then we must be on our guard at all times.'

'What about Hays? Will he help us?' This from Sarah who, despite her fear, couldn't stop eating after so many days on short rations.

To that question too I felt that I knew the answer. 'I believe that if we are attacked in his presence he will feel honour bound to defend us, hence his absence now. Other than that he will follow the instructions of his President.'

'So we really are on our own,' mused the diminutive chargé d'affaires.

'Yes, Charles,' I replied. 'Not for the

first time we are a very thin red line.'

His mind apparently made up, Charles straightened his back and asked briskly, 'So what are your intentions, Thomas? I have no doubt that you have a plan. You always seem to.'

I laughed but kept my voice low. 'Every soldier knows that he is most vulnerable during the hours of darkness. We could make camp with the rangers if they permitted it, but we would still be exposed to ambuscade. So, I propose that we still take up residence on the steamer *Mustang*. Once aboard we can withdraw the planking and remain out of sight. If anyone should attempt to force entry, well then, I shall rely on my shotgun. It has done good service so far.'

Elliot gulped. 'I fear I will not be much help in a battle, but you have my support.'

I turned to Sarah who had at last finished eating. Before I could speak she belched into her hand and said, 'That cooking was so good, I just want to lean back and slap my pappy,'

Despite the circumstances I was unable to contain a grin, and I regarded her with much affection as I spoke. 'I'm not even going to ask what that meant, but I do need to know how you wish to proceed, my dear. Remaining with us could place you in great danger. If you were to take refuge with Hays's Rangers you would most certainly be out of harm's way.'

Her face flushed with anger, which somehow only served to make her more attractive to my eyes. 'No way! After all we've been through, you make a damn stupid suggestion like that? I'm with you for as long as you'll have me, *chéri*.'

'In that case we shall grow old together, my love,' I replied gently.

'If we make it through the night,' added Elliot drily.

Carefully we made our way back to the Brazos River. Dusk was upon us, and I was anxious to get aboard the steamer before dark. My saddle-bags were slung over my shoulder, but I had ensured that my jacket pockets were fairly bulging with pistol balls and percussion caps. A fully charged powder flask hung from a cord around my neck, and I drew comfort from the shotgun in my hands. The dusty streets were thronged with people enjoying the fine evening: men, women and children. The Comanche threat was obviously much reduced here, but I personally could not shake off a feeling of unease. We were not menaced by naked savages this time, but by supposedly civilized fellow white men.

As we approached the river I could make out the great bulk of the steamer facing downstream. Somehow in the failing light it did not look quite so welcoming. The planking connecting ship to shore was still in place, but strangely there were no crew members in sight.

'What captain would leave a ship moored yet unmanned?' This question from Elliot went unanswered as I halted to look along the riverbank. The ranger company appeared to have moved its campsite, for there was no sign of them off to the left, where they had been. Sarah gave an involuntary shiver, and I put my arm around her shoulders. She too could feel it. A sense that things were not as they should be.

'How do you know some folks aren't already aboard waiting on us?' Elliot questioned again.

I tried to sound more certain than I felt. 'If we are to be attacked this night it will be when the city is abed. There will be as few witnesses as possible.'

Hurriedly now we went aboard. There was no shouted challenge, and no crew member came running up to us. The *Mustang* truly appeared deserted. The motion of the ship underfoot felt strange after so long on land. Because it was built for inland waterways, the main deck was very low to the water, and standing there we were almost level with the bank. Grasping the planks I dragged them both inboard and then turned to face the others. 'We need some height. Let's move up to the next deck and find our rooms. We might as well be comfortable.'

Sarah gawped at me. 'Comfortable! When those devils might be trying to kill us. You're plumb crazy.'

I answered that outburst with a broad wink. 'I paid for these staterooms with gold coin, and I'm damn well going to use them.'

Sarah shook her head in amazement and made for the stairs, but I grabbed her arm. 'Charles, I would be much obliged if you would hand your derringer to Sarah. Are you up to using one of these revolvers?'

Reluctantly he nodded and did as I asked. 'The hammer must be cocked before each shot and you have five chambers. Take deliberate aim before you fire.'

Sarah accepted her weapon without any unwillingness. Recalling her with the blunderbuss at the farmhouse door, I had no doubt that she would be able to use it.

Together we made our way up to the next deck. It was rapidly dawning upon me that this would be an awkward craft to defend. The deck was almost all taken up by passenger cabins, with a walkway running around the outside of it, and a flight of stairs on each side of the boat.

Above us was another passenger deck, and atop that the captain's wheelhouse. The higher up we proceeded, the more isolated we would become, and there was a very real danger of the vessel being torched beneath us. However, working on the basis that our every move was being observed, I led the others up to the third and topmost deck. Once there I instructed Elliot to find an axe, possibly in the wheelhouse, and then to join us on the far side of the ship.

Taking Sarah by the hand I headed straight for the nearest cabin, opened the door and pulled her in. I threw down my saddle-bags, pushed her, unresisting, on to the soft double bed and kissed her firmly on the lips. I could taste the spices from the evening meal on her breath as her lips parted, and I knew that, had Elliot not been stumbling around above us, we would have lain there indefinitely. Lust is almost certainly enhanced by fear. For a moment longer we lay there engrossed in each other, until reluctantly I pulled back. Gasping for breath, raven hair spread out across the pillow, she gazed into my eyes. 'You're mad! I love you, but you must be poorly in the head.'

Laughing softly I replied, 'I told you, I've paid for this room and I'm going to enjoy it.' Elliot's footsteps sounded on the stairs. 'But sadly not for long. Come, we must be away.'

Sarah's lips swiftly brushed mine and then we were on our feet. 'Pity,' she whispered, 'I had a hankering to stay put.'

* * *

If Elliot knew what we had been about he did not show it. Ever the diplomat! Proudly he thrust a large axe before him. 'I found this in the wheelhouse, but I can't think why you'd need it.'

Burdened with my shotgun, I replied, 'You keep hold of it. It will be useful if we have to cut the boat adrift.'

Elliot's mouth opened and closed again without emitting any sound. Sarah chuckled quietly, 'Poorly in the head.'

As the passenger cabin straddled the deck, I had made a point of leading us out on the far side, facing the river. My plan was to return to the lower deck unobserved and wait on events at the stern. Anyone watching from the bank would, I hoped, think that we were still on the top deck in one of the cabins, blissfully unaware of any threat. To encourage them in this belief I briefly returned to the room and, using a lucifer, lit two of the oil lamps. The three of us then crept down the two flights of stairs to the lower deck and made our way to the rear. Darkness had fallen, with the moonlight giving an eerie feel to our unfamiliar surroundings. We sat huddled together on the polished deck. Behind us was the huge paddle wheel that propelled the ship by the marvel of steam power. So long as we did not stand up, we would remain invisible to anyone on the shore.

Talking in hushed tones I told my little army what I envisaged for us that night. 'As I see it they have two ways of boarding us. They will either come by boat, or send a swimmer over to replace the gangplank. I believe they will use a boat.'

I could see by the moon's illumination that I had their full attention and so continued: 'If there is just the one boat, I propose that we should rush forward and fire upon it. However, if they send two, we should allow the first party to board and ascend the ship, and then we open fire on the second. We must not permit a boat to remain at large on the river or they could set us afire. If we survive this night I believe that we'll be safe. Houston dare not risk a prolonged fracas in his own capital. He could explain away one incident as the work of river pirates or some such, but if we survive he will have to be seen to act against the conspirators.' It was small comfort, but I felt that I had given them both a ray of hope.

We had sat on the increasingly hard deck planking for at least two hours. I was grateful for the night's warmth, for cold weather would soon have sapped our spirits. The weapons had been checked and checked again, so that all that remained for us to do was to listen. We strained to catch the slightest sound, and had soon learned to discount the repetitive noises created by the flow of the river. The lapping of water against the sides, the creaking mooring ropes and the squeaking of the paddle wheel: all were soon accepted as the norm. So when the warm breeze wafted something slightly different aboard I scurried over to the far side like a startled river rat.

Again I heard it. A very slight plopping sound, as though something was gently disturbing the surface of the water. Inching my way up the ship's wooden side, I took a quick peek over the top and then dropped back. Two rowing boats, one in the lead with four men and the other with three, were moving around the stern. The oars and rowlocks had obviously been well muffled, as their progress was almost silent. I risked another look, as the distance between the two craft was important. Satisfied, I crawled back to where the others anxiously waited.

'Two boats, seven men. There's some distance between them, so we'll let the first unload. If they move upstairs I'll strike the second while you cover me. Understood?'

Grimly they nodded. I smiled at Sarah through the gloom and then, clutching my shotgun, crawled to the back of the rear cabin.

Yet again I was going into action

against greater numbers, but this time I felt strangely calm. I realized that during the long wait I had been unaffected by the usual stomach gripes. Whoever was out there was going to pay dearly for this intrusion!

There was a very slight scraping sound as the first boat came alongside, then a hand appeared at the base of the opening in the side. The assault had begun.

20

One by one, four shadowy figures climbed aboard the *Mustang*. I stood silently waiting, convinced that they must surely hear the sound of my pounding heart. If they were to head aft, instead of up the stairs, we would have to respond rapidly. Behind me Sarah and Elliot were poised, guns at the ready. Hugging the cabin wall I risked a quick glance. Three were moving towards the stairs, whilst one remained at the side awaiting the other boat. Snapping my head back inboard, I rapidly assessed what my left eye had just witnessed. Two of the three heading for the upper decks were carrying shotguns, which was to be expected but boded ill. And the man remaining at the side appeared to have only one arm, *because his right arm was in a sling!*

I'll see you soon, I'll see you soon!

The words resounded in my brain. The wounded assassin from Austin was standing right there in front of me. I could feel my head throbbing as pure rage began to build within me. That man, after attempting to kill Elliot and me outside the hotel, had gratuitously distracted me, knowing that Sarah had already been abducted. Now he was again intent on my destruction, only this time I was going to repay him for his sins. His three companions were either on the second deck or beginning the climb to our cabin. It was time to act. Holding the shotgun in my left hand I drew my hunting knife and took another quick look down the deck. The solitary figure was now peering over the side. The second boat must have arrived.

I drew a deep breath and sprinted down the deck, regardless of who might see me. Distracted by his cronies in the other boat, my prey reacted too slowly to the sound of my footsteps, and I was on him. Blocking his turn with the raised shotgun, I rammed the broad blade of the hunting knife into his belly, so that it was buried right up to the hilt. Uttering an agonized gasp, his eyes widened in horrified recognition as I called out to him, '*Anytime!*'

Shoving hard against him with the shotgun, I sent him reeling through the opening. There was a ghastly sucking noise as his own momentum dragged him off my knife. With a sickening thud he hit the prow of the second rowing boat, before rolling into the Brazos.

I had had my revenge, but there was no time to savour it. Astonished cries came from the boat as I sheathed my bloodied knife, and then pulled back both hammers of the 'two-shoot' gun. Swiftly aiming the weapon, I took in the expressions of pure horror as the awful threat registered with the men before me. A couple reached for their revolvers, but they were too late and knew it. Braced for the shock I squeezed both triggers.

The still night air was torn apart by

the fury of the blast. A lethal spread of lead balls ripped into the three men, and their screams filled the night. With my shoulder aching, and enveloped by smoke, I lurched back towards the stern, anxious to rejoin the others. That sudden movement saved my life.

From the upper deck there came a tremendous roar as another shotgun was discharged, this time aimed at me. The pattern of shot expanded with the distance to include the deck, the assailant's own men and my fleeing silhouette. A searing pain in my right ear caused me to cry out, to be joined by more agonized howls from the hapless occupants of the rowing boat. As I regained the cabin wall I shouted for the others to join me.

'That's four of them out of the fight, leaving three on the upper decks. For God's sake keep under cover. They've got shotguns up there.'

Sarah gasped in shock. 'Thomas, you're hit. There's blood all over you.' Her hand went to my head and came away glistening. 'Those devils have taken part of your ear.'

Before I could respond there came a hail from the riverbank. 'Silas, have you got him? Is he dead?'

'Silas!' The name tore at me like yet another shotgun blast. I hissed at the others, 'How can that be?'

As if in confirmation Braxton's hard voice boomed out from above. 'No, the cockchafer's at the stern along with his bitch.'

'At the what?'

'The back of the poxy boat, you moron! Lay down some fire.'

Desperately I grabbed the others. 'His footpads are hidden amongst the trees,' I hissed at them. 'We must move down to the bow, immediately! It'll give us some time. Go quietly.'

I pushed Sarah and Elliot before me and we moved swiftly down the outside of the boat. As we passed the opening in the side I took a quick look into the rowing boat. Even in the moonlight it vividly resembled a slaughterhouse.

There would be no further danger from that quarter. On reaching the other end of the ship we all crouched down. Rifle fire resounded from the shore, but none of the projectiles came near us. Hastily I reloaded the shotgun, all the while trying to work out our best course of action.

It was Elliot, breathless and quite obviously scared to death, who came up with the idea.

'Let us do what you suggested. Cut the bow adrift. The *Mustang* will stay tethered to the mooring by her stem cable, but the movement of the ship will take us away from the shore and it should certainly confuse those above us.'

'That's a capital idea,' I said, clapping the little man on the shoulder. I pushed home the percussion caps and proffered the weapon to him. 'Hand me that axe and cover me with this. Don't fire unless you are presented with a good target.'

I grabbed the heavy tool and dashed

into the open. The thick rope cable reached over the side and on to the shore. Once that was gone the flow of the river was sure to swing the ship. Knowing that my time before discovery was very limited, I lined the axe up and swung it down hard on to the deck. Splinters flew, and the cable creaked as though in protest. Another swing and I was definitely making progress, but then somebody ashore caught sight of me.

'Silas, the sons of bitches are at the front.'

A shot ripped into the woodwork on the side of the ship, and from an upper deck came the sound of running men.

Desperately I swung again. Nearly through. Another shot rang out, although from where I couldn't tell, and something tugged at my jacket. 'Christ,' I thought, 'this is getting too hot.'

From somewhere close came the tremendous roar of a shotgun discharge, followed by a high-pitched scream. Resisting the temptation to glance round, I took another mighty swing and was through. As the cable slithered off over the side like a demented snake, the ship gave a tremor and began to swing. I darted back to the cabin wall, aware for the first time of the throbbing pain in my right ear. Elliot stood there, holding the smoking shotgun, rubbing his shoulder. 'I think I hit someone, Thomas, but by Jove this thing kicks back.'

Sarah, looking round the cabin wall, back along the offside deck, screamed out a warning. 'They're coming out of the water!'

Taking hurried aim she fired her derringer. I dropped the axe to the deck, drew my revolver and ran to her. Pushing her back out of danger I bellowed, 'Stay with Elliot,' and then threw all caution to the wind. I cocked the hammer and stepped out to confront the new menace, only to find myself facing two opponents. Or was I?

One, the half-caste Huerta, silent as ever, had just leapt down the stairs, shotgun at the ready. The other shadowy figure, fresh from the river and brandishing only a knife, charged straight for him. Finger poised on the trigger, I hesitated, taken aback by the actions of the newcomer. Too late Huerta, sensing the danger, started to turn, but the other man was on him, plunging his blade deep into the Comanchero's neck. With a choking scream the 'breed fell back against the cabin wall. Giving the knife a vicious twist Bannock turned to face me. 'It's a mighty good job you only gave her a popgun, or like as not I'd be dead now.'

Pleasure replaced confusion as I regarded my old companion. About to speak I was interrupted by a harsh yet trembling voice from above. 'That's the last time you use that toadstabber, Beaujolais!'

Even as I looked up there was a tremendous detonation from the top deck. Robbed of my night vision by the flash, I was only partly aware of the ranger being blown backwards, into and then over the rail. There was a splash and he was gone. Bannock's startling reappearance, and then his brutal demise, had been so sudden that I was momentarily stunned. After all that we'd been through, for him to be snuffed out in an instant was just too much. That man had been my friend!

With a howl of anguish I snapped off a wild shot at his killer. Braxton just snarled an oath and stepped back into shadow. On the point of vaulting over the dying Huerta in pursuit, I was abruptly halted by a shouted challenge from the prow, followed by a shot. Turning back, I rounded the corner to find Elliot sprawled on the planking, with Sarah reaching desperately for his discarded shotgun. Across the deck a shadowy figure cocked a revolver and shifted aim. Knowing all too clearly that the man before me would undoubtedly be too quick for her I, calmly and deliberately this time, fired off two aimed shots. As the powder smoke cleared I could see they had hit their mark. Elliot's assailant was slumped unmoving on the deck.

I came up behind the little man, hooked my hands under his shoulders and dragged him back to the relative safety of the cabin wall. He cried out in pain and clawed at me.

'Sarah,' I yelled out. 'See to him while I go after Braxton. He's just murdered Bannock.'

I scooped up Elliot's revolver and handed mine to her, conscious of the shock on her face.

'There are two chambers remaining,' I told her. 'On no account must you leave here. Take care, my darling.'

I kissed her swiftly on her forehead, then scurried over to the man whom I had just killed. Careful scrutiny in the moonlight brought no recognition, but listening to Elliot's low moans I was gratified that he was deceased. As I turned to view the top deck my course of action suddenly became so clear. Braxton was up there, awaiting me. He had no intention of coming for me, preferring instead to let me undertake the harrowing task of finding him. So I therefore had to take the most difficult route, the one he would least expect. That meant using the stairs on the landward side, leaving myself visible to his cronies lining the riverbank. Although the boat had markedly swung out, I would still be under their guns. My mind was made up; I cocked the revolver inside my jacket to muffle the sound, and then began crawling along the deck close to the cabin walls.

Upon reaching the bottom step I launched myself up the flight of stairs. Almost immediately there came a cacophony of noise from the darkened land mass off to my left. I prayed that the swaying of the ship would confuse their aim. Shots and oaths rang out in the night. Lead thwacked into the woodwork and I clearly made out one voice. 'Silas, he's on the deck below you.'

Braxton sensibly remained silent, but I almost laughed aloud at what he must have been thinking. His lackey had helpfully informed me that my quarry was still on the top deck.

Keeping my head down, I crawled along the polished deck away from the stairs. Again I was faced with deciding from which side to ascend. Sweat poured from me as I lay there pondering. I had never been a gambling man, but the risks on this were obvious and I didn't like them one little bit. If I continued up the same side he would be warned from the shore, as his thugs were expecting me now. Therefore he would very probably be waiting on the far side, shotgun cocked and ready. Either way he had the advantage.

Carefully scrutinizing my surroundings I thought, 'There must be another way up!'

Then it came to me. All the cabins had outward-facing windows. If I went round the stern, out of sight of the shore, I could use a window ledge as leverage to climb on to the top deck without mounting either flight of stairs, but it would have to be accomplished swiftly! I tucked the revolver back in my belt, very mindful that it was cocked, and moved swiftly on all fours to the rear of the ship. Carefully keeping myself in shadow I advanced to the far corner. Even with the craft at an angle I was no longer visible to Braxton's cohorts. Gingerly I placed my right foot on the wooden window ledge and tested my weight on it. It seemed firm enough.

I propelled myself upwards, grasped the polished rail and heaved with all my strength. The strain on my arms was truly awful as I struggled to get my body up on to the gently curving rail. At last my head and shoulders were over, followed by my right leg.

Lying prone along the ship's side I was able to see the full length of the deck with all the cabin doors visible. Except one! The cabin where Sarah and I had stolen a kiss was still illuminated, as if to attract me like a moth to a flame. But the cabin before it had just a gaping black hole where the door should have been. I now knew exactly where Braxton was. As he stood in that room, well back from the entrance, the gaping muzzles of his shotgun awaited me.

To try and approach that cabin from either side would be just plain suicide. But there was another way. I could burn him out!

I eased myself very gently on to the deck and crept over to the rearmost cabin. That put me four doors away from Braxton. Cautiously I depressed the handle. Protesting slightly, the door opened. Even having heard that, he would be unlikely to leave his position to investigate. But I had just advertised my presence!

Quickly I reached for an oil lamp and shook it. Satisfied, I crouched on the floor, and shielding the lamp from the riverbank I ignited it with one of my precious lucifers. Keeping the flame almost starved, I came out of the cabin and inched my way towards the open door. The tension mounted unbearably as I got closer, and yet there was exhilaration also. Come what may I was going to avenge my friend who, despite my suspicions, had consistently come to my aid. As I reached the next cabin but one I stopped in horror as a thought struck me. *What if the open door is a ruse de guerre to tempt me?*

Instinctively I dropped to the deck, just as the window glass exploded outwards, showering me with splinters. The roar of the gun in close confinement was terrifying. Miraculously the lamp was still intact, so I turned up the flame and twisted and threw it through the shattered window. There was a sharp crash followed by a burst of flame as the oil ignited. The flames took hold rapidly on the wooden furniture and spread through the cabin. With a howl of dismay Braxton fled through the opposite door. Almost instantaneously there came a fusillade of shots from the shore. I clambered to my feet, drew my Colt and ran for the rear of the steamer, my blood well and truly up. From the opposite side of the ship Braxton was screaming abuse at his marksmen.

'Hold fire, you poxy curs!'

Taking advantage of the chaos I charged round the stern, my revolver levelled, desperately seeking out my enemy. And there he stood, illuminated by the flames surging out of the cabin. The weapon bucked in my hand as I snapped off an ill-judged shot, the ball tearing into timber rather than flesh. What happened next took me totally by surprise.

Rather than seeking cover or even returning fire, the other man drew his knife and ran straight at me. His wounded leg appeared to have little effect on his speed. My heart jumping with shock, I instinctively realized that I had insufficient time to cock and fire again. Taking the only other option, I hurled the piece at his torso and drew my own knife. He swerved slightly to avoid my missile and lost some momentum, which afforded me the chance to see his face in the moonlight.

The sight made me gasp with horror, and brought with it the recollection of Elliot's smoking shotgun. Some of the balls from that discharge had torn into the left side of Braxton's face, gouging and removing flesh. The livid scar had gone entirely, leaving bloodied teeth glistening through the wreckage. He must have been in agony, yet he appeared totally focused on destroying me.

With a triumphant snarl he was upon me, wielding his knife in controlled slashes as he tested my defence. Sparks flew as the blades clashed, and I quickly realized that I was in dire trouble. Knife fighting did not form part of a British officer's training, so I had no experience to fall back on, only sound reflexes. Braxton's razor-sharp blade swirled around me as he searched for a weakness. His eyes were fixed on mine, watching carefully for them to indicate the start of any move that I might contemplate.

I tried kicking and punching, but always he danced backwards before renewing his own attack. Desperately seeking an opening, I dropped my eyes, tossed the knife to my left hand, and punched forward as hard as I could. Taken off guard, he managed to block my blade, but received the blow full on the raw meat that made up the left side of his face. The pain must have been excruciating, for he cried out and fell back, tears flooding from his eyes.

My fist was covered in his blood and I knew that I'd hurt him badly. Unable to resist taunting him, I asked, 'What's become of your duelling scar, Silas?'

Even though in torment he managed a swift, sneering response. ' 'Twas your friend Beaujolais that gave it me, and he paid the price, just as will you!'

So that was behind the hatred between them. Even as the thought touched me I was moving rapidly. Knowing that there could only be one inevitable outcome to the duel of steel,

I lunged for my revolver. It was lying on the deck, dangerously close to the flames that were now spreading to the other cabins on our level. The heat was unbearable, and even as I reached the hot metal I knew I'd made a possibly lethal mistake. With bone-crunching force a leather boot smashed into my right leg, bringing me crashing on to the wooden decking. I still gripped the Colt in my left hand, but was winded by the impact, and I was completely unable to react.

With a harsh laugh, as though belittling my feeble efforts, Braxton kicked hard at the revolver. Unable to maintain my tenuous hold, I watched it skitter off into the flames, lost to me for ever. I felt his fingers thread into my hair, and then searing agony as my head was brutally yanked back. I could just make out the blade as it swept before me to administer the *coup de grâce*.

'Say your prayers, English. Your nine lives are all used up.'

Eyes closed in defeat, I helplessly

awaited the killing stroke. Instead there came a burst of rapid firing, seemingly from within the blazing inferno. All five chambers in my revolver had detonated in the flames. Braxton froze above me, and then turned instinctively towards the source of the noise. Realizing immediately what had happened, I twisted beneath him and swung my right arm in a wide arc. I was still clutching my knife, and the tip of the blade sliced through the bridge of his nose, adding to the agony that was distorting his already ruined face. Releasing his grip on my hair, he surrendered to the shock and fell back. For the second time that night I plunged the knife up to its hilt into an unprotected belly, only this time I gave it a savage twist for good measure. A tremendous shudder travelled through his body as he let loose an inhuman scream. Arms flailing about in reaction to the agony, he sent his own knife flying off into the night, before falling back on to the deck. Sheer relief surged through me, as I realized that at last he was no longer a threat to me.

I sensed rather than heard movement near by, and my gaze drifted away from the terrible sight of him. 'Thomas, are you hurt?' Sarah's lovely form knelt by my side.

'I thought I told you to stay with Charles,' I gasped with a weary smile. 'How's this going to work if you don't do as I say?'

Laughing, we collapsed gratefully into each other's arms, until we could stand the intense heat no longer.

'This is going to take the whole ship, and will highlight us to those ruffians,' I shouted above the roar of the fire. 'We must use the other stairs and somehow get Elliot ashore.'

About to depart but still on my knees, I glanced briefly at the body of the man who had tried so hard to kill me. I recoiled with surprise as his eyes opened.

Speaking desperately slowly he forced out, 'You just won't die, will you?'

'You didn't try hard enough, Silas,' I chided.

'Lamar ain't finished with you yet,' he managed, coughing gobbets of blood on to his shirt.

Despite the overwhelming heat I felt a chill run down my spine, but I still managed a final riposte. 'Well, at least he can't help you any more. You're finished!'

As I pulled away I had the satisfaction of seeing raw fear in the man's eyes: he realized that we intended abandoning him to the flames.

'For pity's sake, shoot me,' he croaked.

Crouching down for fear of the sharpshooters, with my jacket pulled across my face as a shield against the inferno, I called back, 'Would you do that for me, Silas, if the situation was reversed?'

His pain-maddened eyes focused on me as I awaited his reply. It duly came in the form of a gobbet of phlegm hawked on to my trousers.

'Just as I expected,' I commented grimly, before twisting away to join Sarah who was awaiting me impatiently at the stern.

'You took your damn time. He didn't deserve considerations,' she shouted over the noise of the blaze.

'He didn't get any,' I retorted harshly.

* * *

Following a rapid descent of the stairs, we returned to a much weakened Charles Elliot. Blood was visible on the deck and he was deathly pale.

Despite our having survived an attack by seven ruthless desperadoes our situation was, if anything, even more dire. The top deck of the steamer was completely ablaze, with flames now spreading down to the middle one. We had to get off the ship, yet armed men were swarming among the trees set back from the riverbank. Taking in Elliot's condition, Sarah and I viewed each other with grave concern. Both of us knew that we could survive jumping off the far side of the steamer, even if that meant me towing her by the hair again, but Elliot's condition precluded that course of action. The chances of our fighting our way ashore were slim, but seemed the only option. With a sigh of resignation, I commenced reloading the shotgun. The conflagration had turned night into day. Even well to the fore of the lower deck the temperature was rising uncomfortably. The choice of death by fire or gunshot was unenviable.

With the shotgun recharged, I had just moved on to the derringer when an almighty commotion broke out on the shore. Shouts were followed rapidly by gunfire, as if two skirmish lines had engaged. I crawled over to the side of the ship and risked a quick look.

All along the bank I could see men running through the trees, powder flashes offering brief illumination as their firearms discharged. One thing was certain: if the men on land were fighting each other, then neither side was likely to constitute a threat to us. On impulse I stood erect, highlighted for all to see by the blazing superstructure. Sarah leapt to my side, concern etched on her now soot-covered face.

'For pity's sake get down,' she implored.

Grabbing her arms, I shouted over the roaring fire, 'Don't you see, they're too busying warring with each other. We have to get off here *now*, before we're burnt alive. Let's get Charles to the rail.'

Between us we lifted him bodily to the side of the ship. He struggled fitfully, weakened and disoriented by loss of blood. The fire, having by now spread to the bottom deck, had consumed the gangplanks and our escape route was gone.

'Over the side,' I yelled. 'It's our only chance.'

Together we heaved Elliot on to the solid handrail. The cutting of the bowline was now working against us, as the steamer was moving with the current, but there was nothing else for it. Having hurled the shotgun on to the bank, I mounted the rail and plunged in. After the blistering heat, cool water came as a blessed relief.

'Push him in,' I bellowed over the dreadful background noise of gunfire and burning timber. Elliot's body collapsed into the river, but Sarah did not follow. I grabbed him under the chin and pulled for the river's edge. Without the strength to struggle against me, the little man offered no resistance, and we soon covered the few yards. The problem of how to get him ashore was solved when two brawny arms reached down and hauled him out of the water. Startled, I looked up into the grinning face of Ranger Kirby.

'Greetings, Major. You sure know how to cause a ruckus. Is there anything left alive on that?'

'Sarah,' I screamed out. 'Jump in for Christ's sake!'

'I can't swim, Thomas,' she bawled

back, hysteria evident in her voice

'I bloody well know that. Just jump. I'll help you.'

I launched myself across the gap and frantically waved her in. The whole ship was ablaze now and the heat was intolerable. Her choice was either definitely to burn or possibly to drown, so with a wail she threw herself off the side. She disappeared under the glowing surface, only to burst forth seconds later, arms thrashing wildly about. A couple of powerful strokes brought me level with her, and I reached out to seize her arms. Even in such a fraught situation she was ready for me.

'You pull my hair again and I'll drag you down with me, Thomas Collins,' she spluttered breathlessly.

Too weary to reply I swung us around and propelled her towards the riverbank.

Abruptly, without any warning, my head was struck by a massive hammer blow. About to take in air, I was pitched forward under the surface. Water flooded down my throat, and I could feel myself choking. As blackness descended my last thought was: *How can it end like this?*

Epilogue

Slowly, so very slowly, my eyes began to focus. A shadowy figure loomed above me, and I thrust my arms up in a vaguely defensive gesture. A groan escaped my lips as the sudden movement brought on a throbbing ache deep in my skull. Strong but not unkind hands pressed them firmly back on to my chest. Gradually my vision regained its clarity, and with a shock I found myself looking up at Captain John Coffee Hays.

'Welcome back to the living, Major,' he remarked brightly.

He was pushed abruptly aside as Sarah took his place. Her face registered a mixture of affection and concern, but it was no longer coated in soot.

'You took one hell of a sockdologer from that damn boat. I was so fearful

323

that you were dead.'

Vivid memories abruptly crowded in on me. Struggling to sit up, I was hit by a wall of pain and, groaning, sank back on to the blanket. Slowly I managed to form some words.

'What of Charles? Has he? Is h . . . ?'

Sarah cut me short. 'The sawbones fished a ball out of his chest and reckons he'll pull through. He's a tough little cuss and no mistake. Meantime you have to rest. You've been out of it for hours.'

But for the torment in my skull, I would have laughed with joy, but instead I contented myself with a weak smile. Her slim fingers gently swept the hair off my face, where it had settled after my enforced swim.

Doggedly Hays tried again. 'That ruckus you created was enough to wake snakes. The *Mustang* is completely destroyed, along with all its contents, and the captain is demanding recompense from anyone who'll listen.'

Struggling to clear my thoughts, I

gazed up at the diminutive ranger captain. After some moments I was able to formulate a reply.

'Such matters can surely be settled when I again meet with the President?'

Hays had the sensitivity to appear embarrassed as he responded to that. 'There will be no further parley. Houston left for the north at first light. Annexation talks with the US of A continue apace. I greatly fear you were sent here on a fool's errand!'

As the full import of his statement hit me I was completely thunderstruck. All my efforts had come to naught.

'And what of Lamar. Is he free to roam at will also?'

Hays's discomfiture was plain to see. 'Thanks to you there are no longer any witnesses to wrongdoing on his part. The general's reputation remains intact.'

That unwelcome news completed my rout. Thinking it aloud I murmured, 'What am I to do? Where am I to go?'

It was only then that I noticed

Sarah's slim lithe figure was encased in a bright new calico dress. A smile lit up her features as she recognized my interest. Ignoring the ranger captain I struggled to my feet and took her in my arms. A crazy idea was forming in my mind, and with it I abandoned any pretensions to modesty.

Taking her in my arms, I hugged and kissed her until she had to fight me off to gain breath.

'What in tarnation's got you all fired up?' she gasped. 'Not that I'm complaining, mind.'

'I've decided I'm staying in Texas. There's nothing for me in England. I was taken for a fool when I was sent here, and it could have cost me my life. This country is soon to be a part of the United States; there'll be plenty of opportunities. For both of us!'

My heart pounded as I awaited her response. If she laughed in my face, my plans would count for naught. Freezing in my grasp, she stared long and hard before asking, 'You really mean that?

326

You'd stay around this burgh with

'I told you before. I'm not going
lose you a second time.'

'But what'll you do? What'll *we* do?'

She hadn't rebuffed me, which was
all the encouragement I needed.

'I just happen to possess a cheerful
amount of gold coinage, courtesy of the
British Foreign Office. God knows I've
earned it, and it should go a long way
out here. I am minded to accompany
the rangers to San Antonio, if they'll
allow it.'

With that I turned to face the ranger,
who had tactfully withdrawn a few
paces. His thin features wore a broad
smile. Winking at Sarah, I matched his
grin and began to talk myself into a
new future.

'I have matters to discuss with you,
Captain, and perhaps you would call
me by my given name from now on.'

We do hope that you have enjoyed reading this large print book.

Did you know that all of our titles are available for purchase?

We publish a wide range of high quality large print books including:
Romances, Mysteries, Classics
General Fiction
Non Fiction and Westerns

Special interest titles available in large print are:
The Little Oxford Dictionary
Music Book, Song Book
Hymn Book, Service Book

Also available from us courtesy of Oxford University Press:
Young Readers' Dictionary
(large print edition)
Young Readers' Thesaurus
(large print edition)

For further information or a free brochure, please contact us at:
Ulverscroft Large Print Books Ltd.,
The Green, Bradgate Road, Anstey,
Leicester, LE7 7FU, England.
Tel: (00 44) 0116 236 4325
Fax: (00 44) 0116 234 0205

LADY COLT

Steve Hayes

When word comes through that two of the infamous Wallace brothers have been spotted in Indian Territory, Liberty Mercer — only the second woman ever to become a Deputy US Marshal — rides out to arrest them. But things don't go to plan, and Liberty finds herself left in the desert to die. Fortunately, rescue comes in the unlikely shape of a young girl named Clementina, on the run herself — from a stepmother who happens to be the matriarch of the Wallace gang . . .

THE GHOSTS OF POYNTER

Amos Carr

Chase Tyler is headed for the town of Poynter. An attempted ambush, the death of an innocent man and a sheriff who won't play by the rules, added to a brother-in-law who can't be trusted and a young man out for vengeance, all make for a pretty complicated visit. When Chase also meets a woman who bears more than a passing resemblance to his lost love, it would seem there is very little hope of him laying old ghosts to rest . . .